How to Bee

BREN MACDIBBLE

Groundwood Books
House of Anansi Press
Toronto   Berkeley

Published in Canada and the USA in 2020 by Groundwood Books

Groundwood Books / House of Anansi Press
groundwoodbooks.com

We gratefully acknowledge the Government of Canada for its
financial support of our publishing program.

With the participation of the Government of Canada | Canadä
Avec la participation du gouvernement du Canada

Library and Archives Canada Cataloguing in Publication
Title: How to bee / Bren MacDibble.
Names: MacDibble, Bren, author.
Description: Originally published: Crows Nest, NSW, Australia :
Allen & Unwin, 2017.
Identifiers: Canadiana (print) 20190160705 | Canadiana (ebook)
20190160713 | ISBN 9781773064185 (softcover) | ISBN
9781773062143 (EPUB) | ISBN 9781773062150 (Kindle)
Classification: LCC PZ7.M143 Ho 2020 | DDC j823.92—dc23

Cover and text design and typesetting by Joanna Hunt
Printed and bound in Canada

To all the kids who face hard times with courage,
and stand tall for the ones they love.

PEONY PEST

Today! It's here! Bright and real and waiting. The knowing of it bursts into my head so big and sudden, like the crack of morning sun busting through the gap at the top of the door. I fall out of my bunk and hit the packing-box floor. I scramble up, right into Gramps asleep in his chair in front of the potbelly stove.

"Cha!" he growls.

"Sorry, Gramps," I say. "It's bee day." I pull on my pest vest and try to squeeze past him, but he holds out his foot.

"First eat, then bee," he says, real firm. He cuts a wedge from the oatcake on top of the stove.

1

Cockies screech loud from the tree over our shack. They know it's time to get moving.

"I can't," I say and try to squeeze past again. "Foreman's waiting."

My sister, Magnolia, sticks her fluffy head out from the top bunk. "Stomp yourself, Peony-pest," she groans.

"You won't diz me when I'm a bee," I say.

"P the bee? Yeah, dying for that," Mags says and flops back on the bunk. But she won't diz me when I'm a bee. Everyone likes bees. Urbs come out in buses from the city just to see bees work. The Urbs cling to the bus windows as the buses travel up and down between the rows of blossoms, and if they ever look out the back window after they pass me in my boring green pest vest, they'll see me standing there with my rude finger up, telling them how I feel about them getting all the fruit we work so hard to make.

I grab the oatcake from Gramps, duck around him and push through the sacking-lined door.

My chooks cluck when they see me and I flick the catch on the coop door. They push out and peck at the grass.

"I'm not doing pests today," I tell them. "You have to get your own. I'm a bee now." I crumble some of my oatcake, so they cluck all happy around my feet. "Mags is still a pest, she'll find you something to eat." Mags is too big and clumsy to ever be a bee. I take a bite of oatcake and crumble the rest and scatter it so I can get away without chooks on my tail.

Sometimes bees get too big to be up in the branches, sometimes they fall and break their bones. This week both happened and Foreman said, "Tomorrow we'll find two new bees."

ME AND AJ

I race to the meeting point down in apples, but eleven pests are already there. I smile at my friend Applejoy and he smiles back. It's gonna be him and me, like always.

"Peony? Are you ten yet?" Foreman asks when he sees me. His fluffy eyebrows push down towards his nose.

"Yeah, Boz," I lie and look all caz.

He nods, and I join the other kids waiting.

Pomegranate digs me in the back with her pointy finger to tell me she knows I'm lying.

"Cha," I whisper.

Foreman tells us what to do to try out to be a bee. I've seen bees working. I know how it's done. He hands us a leather cord, and when we all have one, Foreman says, "Go!"

The pests rush first to the pile of poles and then to the feather box and scuffle over the feathers. I get my pole and stand back. I don't need those old rummaged-through muck feathers. I reach into my pocket and pull out feathers from my chooks. The best bum fluff. The softest fluffiest feathers. I lash them to the end of my wand just like I seen bees do and then I run to Foreman.

"I done, Boz," I say.

He checks my lashing, nods and hands me a pouch of stamens. He nods towards the trees. "Row one."

I'm proud like I'm gonna bust. This is how I always imagined. Me, first with the lashing.

I run fast down to the apple trees. Pomegranate is right behind me. She got a nod from Foreman and she's running to row two.

I'm light. I'm quick. But Pomz can run along fence tips wide as my thumb. I seen her practising. She's long keen on being a bee.

I scramble into the branches of the first tree. Old, thick and spread wide, easy. I dip my wand into the pouch. The other end tangles in the branches. Pomz dips hers on the ground before she climbs. I'm too stupid for not remembering that's how bees do it. I check over my shoulder. Foreman's busy checking lashings. Maybe he's not seen me do it wrong.

I pull the end of the wand out from the branches and start along a branch. A stick jams in my legs and I trip and fall straight out of the tree. I land on my stomach on the dirt. Pomz sniggers and scrambles up her tree. She's stuck the end of her wand into my legs!

"Cha!" I whisper and scramble to my feet. Foreman don't like bees who fight. He's ripped bee vests right off the backs of bees who fight. I climb back into my tree. Foreman's still busy. Didn't see me fall, but I've lost my lead. Pomz is already doing one side of her tree.

I flick the feathers from flower to flower, every flower I can reach, and coz I'm fast and light and a good climber I can pretty much reach them all. This tree will have lots of fruit soon and Foreman will remember that the first row was the one Peony done.

Pomz is running up the main branches of her tree without hanging on to anything. She's heavier than me but faster coz of her balance. She jumps down and runs to her next tree.

Applejoy has his lashing nodded and he runs past to row four just as I jump from my first tree. "Go, P!" he says.

"Go, Aaj," I say back. I dip the wand in my pouch, with a big show in case Foreman's watching, so he can see I did it proper, before I climb the tree. The pouch is already half empty. I don't know if I'll have enough to finish the whole row. I spilled some when I fell. I don't want to tell Foreman I spilled some, so when he comes to check my skills I just smile.

"Good bee," he says.

I'm full to busting again. I will be a bee today!

THE NEW BEES

Lessons start on the speakers. Urbs don't like that we farm kids are too busy to get educated, so lessons get played over the speakers while we work.

Today's lesson's just for us. It's about the history of the bees. Not us. The real ones they used to have thirty years ago before the famines.

I think they looked like pests. Not the kids who kill pests but the actual bugs. They flew on little wings like some pests from flower to flower to collect nectar to make something sweet like sugar to share with people. "Honey," the speaker says over and over, like honey was the whole point of bees, not this job I'm doing now.

I don't know what honey tastes like. Gramps knows. He says, "Sweet like honey," sometimes. When the real bees flew from flower to flower, they did this job. One tiny bee could do the work of twenty kid bees every day. And the speaker says there used to be millions of them.

I think all the bees went away coz they looked small like pests. Before the famine, farmers didn't have enough farm kids to catch the pests so they sprayed poison on the pests, but the poison didn't know which was bees and which was pests.

Scientists still have some of the little bees and they say one day they'll bring them back to work on the farms.

I don't want the bees to come back. I want to be a bee. Coz Mags and me is farm kids, and we can stay in our shed with Gramps and we get food enough for all of us even though Gramps can't work much no more, except for packing time. Everyone works like a dog at packing time. Little or old, there's so many jobs, everyone works.

Before the famine, Ma was little and lived with Gramps in the city with the Urbs. Life was bad, there was no food and no shed to live in. When the farms came to the city and asked them if they wanted to work just for food and a place to build their shed, they came on the buses with the other people who were tired of living in the streets, and being hungry, and being attacked while they slept.

Ma works back in the city now, coz she says if we don't make some cold hard cash we'll be living in a shed forever. But I like our shed. I like the trees. I like our chooks. If I get chosen to be a bee today everything will be super-cherries.

I jump down and run to the next tree. Pomz is just ahead of me. She looks over her shoulder and scowls a face like a dried apricot that I'm catching her.

There's five trees each in our rows, and when I get to my last tree, there's not enough stamen powder in my pouch to cover the feathers properly. I can pretend, but it's important to get powder on every flower, that I know for sure. If the last tree in my row has no fruit in a few weeks' time, Foreman will be telling me all about it and asking for my bee vest back.

I run two rows down where AJ's in his fourth tree.

"I'm out and I've got one more tree!" I tell him, holding up my pouch. He holds out his and lets me dip. He's a good friend.

"Go! Go!" I tell him and he goes back to work.

Pomz is already in her fifth tree. Foreman's watching

10

us both. We're the leaders. He seen me reload from AJ's pouch. He'll guess I spilled.

I scramble into the tree and get to work, touching each of the flowers gently.

I jump down just after Pomz and we race to Foreman. We arrive together coz I'm faster at running.

Foreman nods and puts Pomz first in line and me behind. That don't mean nothing, I tell myself.

AJ races the girl from row three and beats her to stand in line behind me.

Being first or second doesn't mean you're instant bee. Foreman has to like your style. You have to be gentle to the flowers and branches and not clumsy. With four of us done, Foreman blows his whistle and the other pests run up from their rows to hear who has won. It was one of us four. AJ pats my back. He thinks it's me. I hope it's him as well, not Pomz, coz she's too heavy and mean.

Foreman gets out two new black-and-yellow stripe vests. "The new bees are..." He stops and looks at us all. Me especially. I think my heart is gonna slide out my mouth. "Pomegranate and Applejoy."

I turn around and give AJ a quick hug. I don't let him see my face. "Yay, Aaj," I say but my voice is croaky. I run.

APRICOT SLICES

I get to our shed and slam right into Gramps and I can't tell him what happened coz all I can do is gulp at air and slap at my wet cheeks.

"Shh," he says. "Just too young. Next time." He hugs me tight as he can for a moment, my wet face buried into his smoky shirt.

I am too young. I'm not ten, but I kept up with Pomz and AJ who are. If Pomz hadn't tripped me and made me spill the pouch I'd be first. But she did that coz she knew I was lying about my age. Age is stupid.

Mags is never gonna bee. And with me and Mags growing and needing more food for us and Gramps,

I have to bee soon. Gramps pats my back until I can breathe properly again.

"You and Mags are the best pests the farm's ever seen," he says. "You get back out there and show your spirit. Bees gotta have spirit. Next time they need a bee, Foreman's just gonna call you, straight out."

I nod.

"Mags and the chooks is down in pears today," Gramps says and turns me around and pushes me off.

I wipe my face on my sleeve and walk down to pears.

Mags looks surprised to see me. "Peony," she says like she's breathing out my name. My chooks cluck around my feet. They don't care I'm still a pest after I told them I'd be a bee. They're probably happy. More food for them.

Mags points down the row. "I'm going that way," she says. I pull my skewer out of my vest and check the ground for pest holes, then the trunk, then I scale the branches looking for sap suckers. I find some caterpillars, pluck them off the leaves, cluck to the chooks and drop the caterpillars down to them. The chooks dive on the squirming pests.

I work two rows with Mags before I can tell her.

"Pomz tripped me and I fell out the tree," I say.

Mags leans back against a trunk, wipes her hair from her face and nods. "I knew it was something."

"I ran out of powder and had to get some from AJ. Boz saw me and probably thought I spilled it being clumsy," I say.

"You's never clumsy," Mags says.

"Pomz and AJ got bee," I say.

Mags thinks for a while. "They's good. Not good as you, but."

I take a deep breath and go back to looking for pests. Kids are the best at pest catching, small hands, good eyes, fast and good at climbing. Me and Mags with our five chooks, we're a good team. The chooks keep us fed with eggs, all from the pests we feed them. I dunno how people fed chooks from before when they poisoned the pests.

The farm's full of circles. Bees, flowers, fruit. Pests, chooks, eggs. People, bees, flowers, fruit, pests, chooks, eggs, people…all overlapping circles. I don't understand how it went before the famine. Poison? That's like cutting the circles right through the middle. The circle can't go nowhere but a dead end. No wonder the little bees stopped working and left us to starve.

When the sun gets low, Mags and me follow the chooks home to our shed. Gramps has scavenged apricots from the pulp bin, cut off the bad bits and has some apricot slices waiting for us.

All the good fruit goes to the Urbs in the city, but they won't take fruit with marks on it. So as soon as the fruit appears, adults put paper bags around the fruit while it grows, to keep off the birds and pests and flies. Apples cost loads, so none of us farm kids ever had a whole apple to ourselves. Just bits from the pulp bin on its way to be apple juice. Fruit is my favorite thing in the whole world.

Apricot slices is a treat to make me feel better but none of us say that.

SUPER-CHERRIES

The next morning, I get up and I'm still a pest. I pull on my green vest. I feel like I'll always be a pest.

I go to let the chooks out. AJ's waiting for me outside. His new yellow-and-black vest shines in the morning sun. "Soz, P," he says.

"Nah," I say. "It's Pomz who should say sorry." Then, "You look good."

He grins and runs off to join the other bees. AJ's got a good grin.

I let the chooks out and get them moving in the direction of the trees. Mags catches up to us.

There's a cawing and a yawping kind of screaming

that can only be a flock of cockies. Mags and I run, the chooks scatter and flap in a panic. Coz we're in a panic. There's new fruit on some of the trees and nothing's netted or bagged yet. Even if it is, cockies are smart and will rip off the bags. All our work at keeping the bugs off, all our fruit could be ruined.

A gun blams and a cloud of white cockies rise up complaining and wailing. It's the largest flock of cockies I've ever seen. Squealing around the edges are pink-chested galahs. They wheel and settle again, eyes on the fruit.

Shouting rises over the screams of the birds. Foreman's there with his gun.

"Peony! Get bee wands!" he orders. I sprint for the bee sheds. It's a long way and I'm heaving and gasping for air when I get there.

Pomz blocks the door of the sheds. "Pests can't come in here," she says with her hands on her hips.

"We need bee poles!" I say. I grab her arm and pull her so hard she spins and falls into a group of older bees who are just arriving at the sheds. I rush in, grab a big stack of bee poles and speed back past them all.

"Peony's stealing our wands!" someone shouts. They follow me.

I duck around AJ carrying a box of stamen powder.

"P?" he asks.

"Cockies are attacking the fruit," I gasp.

"Stop her, Applejoy Bee!" someone shouts at AJ.

AJ spins around and makes a show of clumsy stopping me, but he gets in the way of the bees chasing me.

A FOREMAN ONE DAY

When I get back to Foreman, lots of pests are there, flapping their vests at the birds. The bees thunder in behind me.

"I brought all the bees to help, Boz!" I yell at Foreman.

"Good thinking!" he says and orders the bees, "Get up the trees with your poles and whack those thieving cockies!"

The bees look stunned. Bees don't normally help out. Bees like to just do the flowers and nothing else. They think they're the super-cherries, but they can't say now they didn't agree to help. They grab poles and scoot up the trees and beat at the cockies and shout like they're told to. But they look dirty at me and I hang close at the other side of Foreman for a while.

"Why aren't the cockies afraid, Boz?" I ask.

"The drought is really bad up north," he says. "They're starving."

It's sad that we have to fight the cockies for the fruit. But we could starve too if the farm don't make money. And the farm don't make money without fruit. If the farm don't make money we don't get our oats and beans, our new blankets each winter, from Foreman. If the farm don't make money we'll have to leave our shed and move on, and the Urbs won't come to see us with their hand-me-down clothes and hand-me-down toys. Everything we work for will be lost.

Sad as I am for the cockies, I beat at them with a bee pole until they give up screeching and flying and resettling, and whirl up into the sky, an angry ball of cawing, seething white, and move on. That's the way the world is, I guess. Not enough to go around so you got to protect your own. Except it's not ours. It's all bound for the city and the Urbs.

"Thanks, Peony," Foreman says. "Could've lost a lot of baby fruit without your quick work. How's your gramps?"

"He's good," I say.

"I got some jobs for him, cleaning up the packing shed," Foreman says.

"I'll tell him now, Boz!" I say, and I run to AJ and give him my bee pole as Foreman sends all the bees back about their work. I run back to the shed and tell Gramps.

He smiles and hugs my head to his belly. "Foreman likes you, kid. You're a good worker and you make this family look good." He picks my face up in his hands and smacks a big funny kiss on my forehead.

I'm full to busting as I head on back to where me and Mags was in pears yesterday. I pull out my skewer and round up the chooks who are scritching and pecking about under a passionfruit vine where they thought the crazy cockies couldn't see them. They think any big bird in the sky is an eagle come to eat them. I don't know that any of these chooks even seen an eagle, but the idea is born into their brains. Chooks is born being chooks and that's all they'll ever be. Not like a dog, which could be a sheep dog, or a cow dog, or a guard dog, or a dog that pulls a blind person around. Not like a girl that's born in a shed and crawls around in the dirt till she learns to be a pest, and then could be a bee or a bagger or picker, or even a foreman one day.

FULL OF TIRED TALK

Ma comes back from the city for her weekend off. I see her from the last pear tree in the row. Her shoulders are hunched and she's dragging her toes in the dust as she climbs the hill from the highway to the farm. Pomz's big sister is walking ahead of her, swinging her arms and taking bouncy steps.

"It's Ma!" I tell Mags.

"I'll finish and bring the chooks back," Mags offers and I set off galloping down the hill, lifting my feet high so the grass heads don't whip and sting my knees. Mags can't run fast like this, but she knows I love to.

I reach Ma and skid to a stop, kicking up dust, and

wrap my arms around her waist in a giant hug.

"Peony!" Ma says. "I didn't see you coming. You scared me to death, almost!" I look up at her laughing and then stop. One of her eyes has a black ring around it and her cheek is all swole up like she banged it.

"What happened to your face, Ma?" I ask.

"Oh nuthin', blossom," she says. "Just a wall and me had a difference of opinion."

I take her bag and sling it over my shoulder, then take her hand and tow her up the road like I'm the ma and she's the little one. Her hand is wrinkled and rough like she's been working real hard. Her fingernails, all cracked and snaggy, scratch at my T-shirt when I pull her hand in close.

"You're getting so tall and strong, P," Ma says.

"I'm real close to being a bee," I tell her. When I look back over my shoulder, her eyes don't light up like I want. One's red-veined and watery, and the other is just doing its regular thing, being a nice brown color, but reflecting the late afternoon sun, so it looks glassy and breakable.

My mother pads along behind me for a while. "You know there's other jobs in the city for strong smart girls like you," she says, like being a bee is nuthin'.

23

I shake my head. "Cha! I don't wanna live in the city with all those greedy Urbs. I like it here. I'm gonna be a bee soon, and one day I'll be a foreman."

"A foreman?" Ma says, all surprised.

I nod. "I know everything about the farm. I know every single job. I been paying attention."

Ma laughs. "You'll never be a foreman," she says, like she knows something I don't. "You don't need to work on the farm," she says.

"Not going to the city," I tell her. "No way." She laughs and messes my hair like I'm being silly.

When we get to the shed and Gramps sees Ma's face, his eyebrows rise in peaks and Ma walks to him and leans into his chest and cries.

Gramps hugs her and strokes her hair and says, "Rosie, honey sweet."

I take Ma's bag into the shed and put it on the table and tidy up my bunk for Ma. This is how it goes. Ma comes home dog tired and crying, and Gramps feeds her tea and oatcake with apricot pieces and puts her to bed in my bunk. I'll sleep with Mags tonight so I don't disturb Ma while she catches up her sleep. And in the morning she'll open that bag of hers and pull out more tea and some lollies and maybe even a banana, then she'll press actual cash into Gramp's hands. Cash that the Urbs use to buy stuff, but there's never anything to buy out here so Gramps hides it in a little metal box under the packing-crate floor.

"Please, Rosie," Gramps says as he sits her down in his chair in front of the stove. "Don't go back this time. Stay with us. All three of us are working now. We need someone to collect firewood and make oatcakes and maybe grow some veggies for us." Gramps pours her some tea. "We have enough food to make it through to picking season. Just stay."

"Stay, Ma," I say.

The sacking over the door pulls back, letting in bright shafts of light, and Mags steps in and lets it drop. She looks at Ma already in the chair with wet cheeks and her eye all black and she goes to her and kneels at her feet and hugs her around the middle. Then she relaxes off a bit and rests her head in Ma's lap.

Ma strokes Mag's fluffy dark hair. "I have to go back," she says softly. "And I'm taking Peony with me."

Mags pulls her head out of Ma's lap. Gramps looks at me quickly. I shake my head.

"No," Gramps says. "It's better for P to be here in the fresh air and sunshine."

Ma shakes her head. "She can work for cash in the city."

"Shh, now," Gramps says and he hugs Ma's head to his middle. "You need to sleep, my honey sweet." He helps her up and bundles her into my bunk. I pull up the blanket to her shoulder, then I turn to Gramps.

"No way," I whisper.

Gramps smiles softly and pushes me outside. "She's just full of tired talk. You ain't going nowhere," he whispers.

We eat our dinner of beans in sauce on the packing boxes out front with Applejoy, who's got his little brother, Mangojoy, on his lap while his mother spoons food into MJ's cherry-blossom mouth.

Gramps scrambles up some eggs for MJ and tells AJ's mum to eat some as well. AJ's mum is real skinny. Her skin stretches over her bones and she wears too many layers of greyed and fraying clothes against a chill that ain't there. It looks like just lifting food into her baby's waiting mouth is hard work for her. That's why I'm pleased AJ is a bee and will get more food to feed her and little MJ.

Gramps gives Applejoy an oatcake with pieces of apricot in it and a sprinkle of sugar on top. A special treat for Ma coming home, even though she's always straight to bed. AJ shares it with little MJ while his mother goes back to their shed to rest. AJ looks after her with his face puckered like a burr on a tree trunk. I move close to him and take little MJ's sticky palm and blow raspberries into it to make him giggle. Nothing is funnier than a giggling baby and soon we're all laughing. AJ has a good laugh.

RED SHOES

I wake in the night and our shed is full of whispering.

"Think what you're saying," Gramps whispers. "She's only nine. Why not Mags?"

"You think those Urbs want a kid like Mags around?" Ma says. "You think they want to look at her dragging her turned-in foot, and she don't know when to shut up and just work. You want to see her get blapped across the face daily for smart-mouthing?"

"I don't wanna see either of them go," Gramps says.

"Peony knows when to shut up. She knows how to work hard. She's smart so won't get into trouble like Mags or me," Ma says.

"She's happy here. She's one of Foreman's favorite farm kids. We need her here," Gramps says.

"She'll do good anywhere, and she's my kid so I say what goes," Ma whispers.

Gramps don't argue with that. He's doesn't yell that Ma ain't ever here so she don't see how good it is and she don't get to say where I go. He just shuts up.

I want to yell at her, but like she said, I know when to shut up. I turn over to see if Mags has heard. Mags strokes my face like she's sorry I have to go, and then she pulls my nose coz she's gotta diz me for things to be normal. I ram my knee into her stomach and turn back away to sleep, but it don't come easy.

When it comes time for Ma to go back to the city, she gets up early, packs my good black trousers I never wear into her bag, wraps her hand tight around my wrist and heads down the path without a word of goodbye to Gramps or Mags. Not even looking at Gramps when he says, "Rosie, please. Rosie, leave her with me. It's safer here for her."

Foreman's standing outside the packing shed and he sees her dragging me along. "Don't you take that little girl to the city," he tells her.

Ma sticks her nose up in the air like she's sniffing the clouds and keeps walking.

"S'okay, Boz," I say. "I jus' gonna see what it's like in the city." I give Foreman a nice smile.

Foreman shakes his head.

Ma gets me all the way down to the road and I'm skipping along beside her like I'm all super-cherries about going down to the highway to meet the bus.

"Will I have to wear shoes in the city?" I ask Ma.

"Yes, P," she says.

"Can I have red shoes?" I ask.

"Yes, P," she says.

"Let's go then," I say and I pull her along up the dusty road. The bus rumbles over the rise in the distance. "Run, Ma! The bus!" I say and pull her again. "Pomegranate's sister is gonna catch the bus and we're gonna miss it!" I yell. She trusts me then and her rough-skin hand slides off my wrist. I run on ahead and she follows. The bus stops ahead of us and I run around the back of it with her following. Pomz's sister is just getting on.

"Ma!" I say as she rounds the back of the bus too. "I don't wanna wear shoes and I don't wanna be blapped across the face." I take off around the front of the bus, back across the road and light out across the paddock, back up the hill towards the orchard.

"P! Peony!" Ma screams after me, but she can't catch me

running uphill. This is why I always gotta live somewhere out in the open, where I can run to be safe.

In my imagination, everyone piles off the bus to chase me, and every one of those people is an Olympic sprinter, but when I check back over my shoulder, it's just my ma standing in the road screaming my name. I slow down. She can't not get on the bus. She's due back to work. I keep moving away so she doesn't think I'll change my mind. She throws her hands up and gets on the bus. I stop and wave as the bus grinds through the gears and carries her away.

Foreman tilts his head when I get back and laughs.

Mags runs to meet me, hop-running just fine on her turned-in foot, with chickens flapping and squawking after her not knowing what the panic is about. She hugs me.

"P! You little pest!" she says.

"I told her I wasn't goin'," I say.

Mags lets me go and as we walk back up to our shed she shoves me sideways, sets me stumbling off the path coz that's normal, and I jump back on the path and shove her off so she almost trips over a chook.

"She's gonna be so mad next month when she comes home," Mags warns.

31

I shrug. "That's a long time away," I say.

Gramps is waiting and smiling sadly. He wipes a tear from his eye and wraps me in a hug. "My little honey girl," he whispers. "Don't you ever leave me."

"I won't, Gramps," I say.

REAL COOKIES

The next time I see Ma dragging her feet through the dust heading uphill to the farm, I don't run and meet her. I tell Mags I see her and can she take the chickens home and then I head off to the packing shed. I scale the inside wall and sit up in the rafters where no one can reach me. Right up near the hot tin roof. Foreman comes in and he sees me sitting up there right in the middle of the packing shed.

"You stuck?" he asks.

I shake my head.

He thinks a moment. "Your ma back from the city?" he asks.

I nod.

He nods like he understands and heads off. He comes back a while later and he's got a paper bag, like what the baggers put around the fruit to stop it getting marks. He throws it up to me without saying nuthin'. I catch it. He winks and leaves.

I open the bag and inside are three oat cookies. Actual cookies cooked in an oven, not just pot-cooked oatcake. And they're real sweet like they're made with syrup, and they've got raisins in them. That Foreman, he lives like a king, proper house, proper oven, amazing food. One day I'll be foreman and have all this stuff too.

I stay up there in the rafters with the heat of the tin roof making me sleepy till it's well dark, then I climb down and sneak home and slide through the sacking door. Gramps is leaned back in his chair, his eyes reflect the crack of moonlight coming from the door. I go to Ma already asleep in my bunk, and lean in and kiss her cheek. It's salty wet. Then I go to Gramps and lay my head on his chest, warm through his raggedy jumper. He grabs me like he can't hold me tight enough. But he don't have to hold me. I ain't goin' nowhere.

I climb up onto the top bunk with Mags and roll her over so she's on the outside edge where I normally sleep and I'm inside against the wall where Ma can't grab me easy.

And that's just what she does real early. She gets up and sees a fluffy dark head where I normally sleep and grabs Mags by the arm.

Mags moans and pushes me awake, before she's pulled off the edge of the bunk. I scramble up and slide off the end of the bunk as Mags crashes down on Ma. I duck under the table and crawl out the door and run.

"Peony!" Ma screams, waking up everyone as she chases me down past Applejoy's, past Blossompink's, past Pomegranate's, around fire pits and packing-box seats, and finally gives up. I keep running till I pass all the worker sheds then I double back and sneak behind the sheds, picking my way around firewood stacks and bits of spare building rubbish, and trees that stink of wee, till I get to Applejoy's, where I sit on his firewood stack to listen to Ma who's still screaming.

"You think I want to wind up like Lily next door, wearing rags, and sick and starving, and having no money for medicine?" Ma yells and I hope AJ's ma is still asleep, but MJ's grizzling behind me so I reckon she's heard. "It's not fair that I'm the only one working in this family when Peony can earn money as well!"

"P and Mags work hard for their food and board," Gramps says. "They're good kids and we have a good life here. We don't need money."

"Today, but what about tomorrow? What about when they're big and you're sick or dead, old man!" Ma yells.

"Rosie!" Gramps says.

"What about me?" Ma says. "When will my life get easier?" Ma breaks down sobbing.

"Rosie, honey sweet," Gramps whispers. "Stay with us."

"Stay here with us, Ma," Mags says.

A stick cracks beside me and I jump. AJ stands there, looking at me. His eyes are shiny wet. I reach out and pull him down to sit on the stack beside me. He sits and squeezes my hand like he's trying to make me feel better, but my ma's the one that's being mean about his ma so I squeeze his hand right back.

I stay out of her way all day, don't get no food, and after dark, cold and hungry and so miserable I could cry, I crawl into AJ's shed and tap him on the shoulder.

He leans out of his bunk and blinks at me. "Come up," he whispers and I climb up and crawl under his blanket next to him. At least I'm warm, and tomorrow morning Ma will go back to the city and Gramps will feed me oatcake for breakfast.

TALKING TO BITUMEN

A little voice from far away is calling me. "P? P! Peony!"

Applejoy shakes me awake. "Aaj?" I moan and open my eyes.

The little voice is going on far away. AJ is up, standing, puffing like he's been running, eyes all panicky. "She's taking Magnolia instead," AJ says.

"Mags!" I throw the blanket off and fall out of the bunk. Scramble up and run. Down the path, out onto the dusty road, to Gramps standing there, staring down the road. "Peony!" he says.

Ma is dragging Mags, too fast, her feet are kicking up dust as she stumbles, looking back. "Peony!" Mags screams.

And the bus is rumbling over the rise in the distance. I run. I run as fast as I can. My feet are moving so fast they're slipping on the dirt under me as they touch and push. My chest is bursting with the effort, but I need to go faster.

The bus pulls up. Ma drags Mags around the back of the bus. Mags looks back at me one last time, reaches for me. I'm not going to make it. But the bus doesn't pull away. The bus waits. And I reach it and run around the back, and Mags is lodged there. Her feet either side of the doorway as Ma pulls her arm, and thumps her hand to make her let go and screams at her. I run and grab Mags around the waist, pull her back.

"Let her go!" I scream.

"No!" Ma says. "You come instead!"

"No!" I say, and Ma pushes Mags on top of me, steps out, leans down and latches on to my foot.

Mags scrambles up and grabs my arm, pulls me back. Then she gets a fire in her eyes. Her face sets hard. She lets go of my hand, makes a fist and rips her arm from across her body up, up, connecting the back of her hand with Ma's cheek and then on up into the air. Ma's head snaps back and she falls onto the bus steps.

I scramble up, grab Mags around the waist, pull her away.

Ma shakes her head, sits herself up and rubs the side of her face. She looks up at us and scowls and stands slowly.

I can't believe Mags just blapped our ma across the face like some nasty Urb boss.

Ma steps back onto the bus step. "I wash my hands of you," she says. "You're dead to me now."

The bus door shuts and the bus lurches off with Ma staring dagger eyes back at us.

Mags drops to her knees, sits in the dirt, tears dripping down her face even though she's not sobbing.

I stroke her shoulder. "Mags," I whisper.

She sniffs. "She don't want me at all," Mags says to the crumbly edge of the bitumen road. "She just wants you."

"Soz, Mags," I say, like it's my fault. I squat down on my heels in front of her. Try to look in her downward eyes. "She don't know how strong you are," I whisper and slide my hand into Mag's hand, limp in her lap. I pick it up and squeeze it tight.

"She ain't coming back," Mags says to the road. "And it's my fault."

"No," I say. "She don't mean it. She's jus' angry. She jus' talks bad when she's angry." I pull Mag's hand and

39

help her to her feet. I brush the dirt and stones off her bare knees, and from a graze on her elbow where she fell back. Then I lead her back across the bitumen and up our dirt road to where Gramps waits with his arms out wide and red-ringed eyes.

GOOD PUPPY

Ma don't come back right through the rest of spring and into the long hot summer. I don't mind coz I'm still mad at her, but Gramps and Mags is sad.

Gramps is sad coz Rosie used to be his little girl before Mags and me. Mags is sad coz she thinks it's her fault Ma ain't coming home. I know it's my fault but I keep telling myself I don't care. Summer is so busy with picking and packing and trucks all coming and going that none of us really has time to do much worrying.

Foreman stomps about bossin' and orderin' and we're all working from sun-up to sun-down just to get the trucks loaded and off on time. We crash asleep each night and stumble back to the packing shed the next morning, wiping the sleep from our eyes still.

Gramps wakes us and feeds us eggs as well as oatcakes each morning to keep us strong, and Foreman feeds us cans of fish and potato fries at lunch, and gives us sweet drinks to be going on with so we're eating like kings and working like dogs.

Mornings, me and Mags put the packing crates together from stacks of pre-cut bits of wood. Just two ends stamped with a green pear and two orange apricots and some words, and a pile of longer bits that we tack between the ends: two each side, three across the bottom. We have small hammers and real sharp long staples. We sit on the floor and work on them between our knees, spitting the staples from our lips as we need them and tacking them together in a tappety-tap dance.

Sometimes the older packing women sing. They sing songs of lost loves and cities far far away. I don't really understand them, but Mags sometimes belts out the middle bits that repeat all the time, her voice slow and achey like a long hot summer. I tap along with my little hammer. Then we pass the crates to Blossompink, who's only five, to carry to the stack next to the packing tables. She wipes the sweat from her forehead and carries them two at a time with her tongue all sticking out sideways. She's real pleased she's got an important job. Afternoons, we run about restocking cardboard trays and tissue paper for the packers and making sure the packed trays all get outside ready for the trucks. The trucks rock up with big canvas walls stamped with a giant picture same as the crate ends. The green pear and the apricots.

Late afternoon, our feet are dragging so much we're snagging our toenails. Still, it's a super-cherry summer with all of us working alongside each other and chatting in the packing house like a big family, and all the trucks are loaded and drivers go off happy.

The bees are in the trees in the morning and the packing house in the afternoon. Which is good coz I get to see AJ, but bad coz Pomz is always sticking out her foot to trip me whenever I pass her.

I soon figure out she's not watching her packing box when she's watching for my foot, so what I do is, I reach over and drag her pile of tissue paper for wrapping the fruit right to the edge of the packing table. I wait until Foreman is nearby and purposely walk past her and make a big show of tripping over her foot.

She laughs as she spins back to the packing table and that's when all the pretty purple sheets of tissue paper

43

catch her elbow and fly across the packing room. Floating and wafting on the air from the fans in a glorious show, like giant blossom petals in the wind. Pomz's silly snigger turns to an open mouth and she turns to face Foreman.

"Pick those up!" he says to her, his eyes thin cracks, saying she's too careless.

"Yes, Boz," she says.

Foreman strides off.

"Yes, Boz," I whisper at her and smile.

The work lets up as the summer goes on, and Foreman puts a pig on a roasting spit to celebrate. I dunno what's higher than a king, but holding a hunk of fine oat bun with a pile of white baked meat, soft and falling apart in my mouth, juice running down my chin, I'm eating like that. Higher than a king.

Gradually we drift off from watching the coals of the roasting pit back towards our sheds, nice and early for a change. Mags is already gone home and I'm walking with AJ who is carrying a bone and gnawing the meat off like a dog.

"Good puppy!" I say to him to make him grin his excellent grin.

There is a car in the driveway, a flash silver car, with red dirt up its sides from our dusty road. It's revving and a guy leans out looking for someone. We laugh at him hanging out of his car like a big old ape, and he lets the car go skidding forwards a bit, kicking up dust and stones that ping off the shed behind us.

We run away and laugh again at how stupid he is.

There's a bang in our hut ahead of me, and Ma yells, "Stay down there, you gimp!" I bust in past the sacking door and Mags is on the floor with a fat lip, wiping the blood off it. Ma is standing there holding Gramps's tin box of money.

MA BROKE HER

"It's my money!" Ma says like I'm going to stop her and pushes past me and marches down the path.

I run after her. "We don't want your stupid money!" I yell. "Take it! Go away! We don't care!"

Ma stops and turns back to me. "I'm gonna be married, Peony. I'm gonna be married and have a baby and live in a real little house." Ma's stomach is a small mound. "And you can come and be part of a real family, with me." She holds out her hand like she don't know me at all. Like she expects me to take it.

"I am part of a real family!" I scream at her and run away back to Mags on the floor of our shed. The car roars off down the driveway, tires skidding and gravel rattling, and then down the road. Mags is sobbing and she won't stop no matter how much I hug her and tell her it's okay.

It's like Ma broke her.

"She's stupid and she's wrong," I say to Mags. Mags won't lift her head out of her knees. I have to get Gramps. AJ's standing there with his mouth open and I tell him to pat Mags on the back while I'm gone and I run out the door. It's dusk now, so Gramps will be home soon anyway.

Someone steps out of the trees and grabs me and wraps a huge hand over my mouth so I can't scream. He's big and strong and carries me kicking and struggling and yelling into his palm down to the road.

I bite his big fat hand, and he lets my mouth go, so I scream, but he blaps me across my face so hard that bright lights swim in my eyes. He wraps his hand over my face again.

"I didn't wanna hurt you," he growls in my ear. "You made me do that. You tell your mother it was your fault. I dunno why she wants you at all."

He carries me down the road like I weigh nothing and lets go of my mouth again to open the back door of the car. I scream again as he shoves me into the back seat and Ma's arms, and slams the door.

I push Ma off, still screaming, and struggle with the door, but it's locked. I scramble to get over the front but Ma pulls me down. I punch her and kick her off, still screaming as the Ape man pulls the driver door open and gets in.

"Shut her up!" he yells. But I won't shut up. I scream like I have lungs the size of a packing shed as he starts the car. I scramble towards the front passenger seat. The Ape slaps me back, grabs the seat headrest beside him and swivels back to look at Ma and me. His bottom lip presses up into his top lip making his chin lumpy. His eyes squint hard at Ma. "You shut her up, or I'll have to!" he yells.

Ma wraps her skinny hand over my mouth, digs her nails into my face and pulls my ear to her mouth. "Don't make him mad, P!" she whispers, like she's more scared than me. "Please!" she begs me. The car takes off down the road, stones banging up against the floor. I rip Ma's hand off my face and scream at her.

The Ape man stomps on the brakes so hard Ma and me slap into the seats in front. Then he turns back and, as I scramble away, he smacks me in the back of the head so hard, my forehead smashes into Ma's chin.

"Shut up!" he yells and takes off down the road again.

I push myself into the corner of the back seat as far as possible away from Ma and the Ape.

Ma rubs her chin and looks at me. "Peony," she whispers. "You might hate me now, but it's for the best. You're going to love being part of our family. You can help me with the baby, and the housework. We'll finally be happy."

"I was happy!" I growl.

I have a headache and I'm so tired from working all day and eating pig meat, that even though I try to count the turns and direction of the car, as the night gets darker and darker outside, I lose track and fall asleep.

WIDE YELLOW SEA

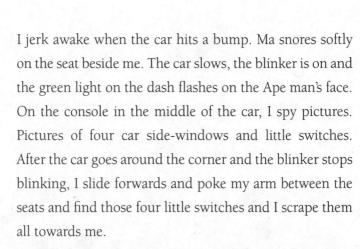

I jerk awake when the car hits a bump. Ma snores softly on the seat beside me. The car slows, the blinker is on and the green light on the dash flashes on the Ape man's face. On the console in the middle of the car, I spy pictures. Pictures of four car side-windows and little switches. After the car goes around the corner and the blinker stops blinking, I slide forwards and poke my arm between the seats and find those four little switches and I scrape them all towards me.

All the windows go down, and the wind roars in, and the Ape looks around like he can't understand why, until he sees my arm and he slaps it away, but I'm already

50

scrambling back and out my window. And he's stomping on the brakes, and growling, and reaching back for me, but I'm hanging on to the window frame and swivelling my legs out the window as well, until just my bum is in the car and the rest of me is out, clinging, ready to jump, soon as the car gets slow enough.

"Peeee!" Ma yells and snags my shorts, but I push off with my legs and hands against the side of the car and leap. I hit the road, slam my hip and shoulder and slap my temple and roll, skinning my elbows and knees, and one ankle, but I'm up and running down into the ditch and over the fence that sits on the other side and off into the paddock as the car turns about and lights up the paddock beside me. Ma and the Ape open car doors and yell and scream my name. I run and run, past where the car lights can reach. My feet got scraped when I jumped, and every footfall on the dry grass scrapes them some more, but I don't care.

The fence creaks way behind me, and I trip and tumble on my chin in the dirt. And though my knee is stinging like I ripped it open and my chin is aching like I grazed it, I keep on running across that dark paddock. I hit a line of trees, run along it, and choose one tree and climb it, up and up, above the reach of the Ape. I wrap

51

my body around it, like I am the tree and the tree is me, and hang on.

Footsteps thud past, and then a while later thud back again. "She's gone!" the Ape says.

Ma's crying. "No," she says. "She's just a little girl. We can't leave her out here in the middle of nowhere," she says, like she knows he don't care about finding me. "Peony!" she wails.

I don't answer.

"Peony!" the man yells. "Come out and we'll take you back to the farm!"

I don't answer. I don't believe him.

"Maybe she's hurt from the fall!" Ma says.

"Come back to the car," the Ape says to Ma. "We'll sleep in it and look for her when the sun comes up."

I wait a long time after they leave. I wait for a break in the clouds above, for the moon to come out and shine on the paddock, then I get down out of the tree and walk, away from the car and back in the direction I think we came from. I walk all the way through to morning and then when the sun comes up I find a creek for a drink and crawl under the bank beside it and sleep. I wake up hot and sweaty and wade into the creek. My T-shirt is torn and I have grazes on my shoulder, my knee, my shin as well as my feet. My chin burns in the cold water as I wash my face. I wash all my grazes, drink the cool water, and walk up the creek, stepping carefully on the rocks or on the flat mud beside the creek.

The car sounds off in the distance, and Ma's yelling. It sends me dropping into the grass on my belly, but they haven't seen me. I guess they're driving up and down looking for me still, but I'd rather be out here lost, than in that car with them. Why won't they just give up? I pick up a rock and hurl it in the direction of their voices. I show them the rude finger. I want to swear at them but I'm afraid they'll hear, so I get up and run.

Running through this tall grass, bent low, is like swimming in a wide yellow sea. The grass heads whip and sting at my face, and neck and eyes, and it's hard to see where I'm going and my feet burn and ache, but I can't stop coz the car is louder now. I throw myself through the grass with one hand up over my face so the stalks whip at my arm instead. Still the car gets louder. Then a new sound. A whipping of thousands of little grass heads on metal. A kind of brrrrring. My breath runs all out of my lungs at once. The car is in the yellow sea with me!

Tires skid, car doors bang and feet pound. "PEEEony!"

the Ape booms like he's calling me from a mountaintop, but he's right here, feet pounding, behind me.

"Peony!" Ma screams.

The Ape snags my shirt, hauls me up in the air, wraps his meaty arms around me as I kick and claw and scream.

Ma arrives, tears running down her face. "Peony, baby, you were running in circles!" she says.

The wide yellow sea tricked me. Even the wide yellow sea is against me. I cry then. I give up and let them put me in the car.

THE RAGGY PEOPLE

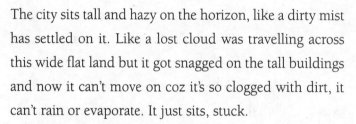

The city sits tall and hazy on the horizon, like a dirty mist has settled on it. Like a lost cloud was travelling across this wide flat land but it got snagged on the tall buildings and now it can't move on coz it's so clogged with dirt, it can't rain or evaporate. It just sits, stuck.

"There it is!" Ma says, like it's a pretty flower or a perfect fruit, not some stupid pile of dark buildings with a stuck cloud.

I scrunch back into my corner away from her and pretend to sleep.

The car stops at a crossroads. There's a rush of raggy people towards the window. Dirty hands hammer at the glass. I pull myself out of my squashed-in corner and slide to the middle of the seat. They'll rip the door off and I'll tumble out and be trampled for sure.

"What do they want?" I whisper to Ma. I dunno if she can hear me over the cawing of the voices calling to us. An old woman pushes her nose white against the glass beside Ma, her grey hair dark and greasy. "Missus, missus, please!" she calls.

The Ape swivels in his front seat like maybe he's going to slap my legs again and I pull them up to my chest, but he's scowling at the people.

"Clear off!" he yells at the windows, then mumbles, "If they scratch Niko's car, he'll murder me." And the hands slide off, trailing down the glass leaving dampness that fades to streaks.

On my knees, pulling on the back of the seat to lift my eyes level with the rear window, I'm glad the raggy people move on to the car behind us, like a mob of shooed-off blowies buzzing on to the next bit of food, but reaching hands limp, like they know they'll get nuthin', eyes wide and sad, dark lines of dirt in the folds of their skin.

Ma pats my back. "They're jus' hungry," she says. "They think we got money coz we borrowed this nice car." I shake her hand off me. I'm still mad at her.

There's a beep, a door lock pops open, and there's the creak of a door. The Ape's door. An angry fat head shoves into the car. A black leather arm rips the key from its socket. The car dies. A pair of big meaty hands wrap around the Ape's throat and drag him from the car.

Ma squeals and dives over the front seat after him, crawling from the car. "Niko, please!" she says.

The fat-head man holds the Ape out on the end of one arm and yells something about his car. The Ape don't fight, he just waves his hands and says he's sorry and things got delayed and he knows he should'a got the car back sooner. And Ma pleads too, grizzling like a baby, breaking down in a way I never seen before. She goes to grab Fat Head's fist as it launches at Ape, but it powers right through her skinny fingers like they're nothing but wing feathers. The Ape's head snaps back.

I crawl over the seat to the front, to get out too. Maybe to run, but I stop, coz the Ape is on his feet and he's counting out cash, folding some into a wad, offering it over, saying, "I'll pay for the extra time." Ma's cash. From our tin!

Fat Head takes the money and blaps the Ape in the mouth so hard he falls down again.

"If you had any sense, you'd stay down!" Fat Head

growls, standing over him, fist smeared with red, ready to knock him down again.

"Yeah, I think I'll do that," the Ape mutters through his fat lip and spits blood-speckled foam onto the tar of the road.

Fat Head turns back to the car, sees me, and grabs me by my shorts waistband and pulls me out of the car. "Get out of my car!" he yells like maybe I'm one of the raggy people who just got in here by mistake.

"Cha!" I yell and beat at his arm till he drops me. I scramble over the Ape and take off, but wham straight into the old woman. A sour stench hits my throat, makes me cough as I push back from her. Ma wraps her arms around me. The car takes off in a roar and leaves us standing in the street with the raggy people all turning to look at us. They stick their dirty lined hands out at us and shuffle back our way. They seen the money tin from inside the Ape's jacket.

Right now, I'm glad for my ma's two skinny arms wrapped around me so tight I almost can't breathe.

WE DON'T BELONG

"Come on!" Ma says as she unravels one arm from me and hauls at the Ape's shoulder sleeve.

The crowd of raggy people is shuffling in a circle, building a wall around us.

I look up at the old woman with the greasy hair and she steps away making a path out, and tilts her head like she's saying, "What yer waiting for?" Ma and me take off up the street with the Ape staggering behind.

We stick close to the speeding cars, not the buildings, coz the doorways are full of people sitting and waiting like spiders in webs of trash.

It makes me think of Gramps's stories about before

he came to the farm. Him telling Ma I'd be safer at the farm. This is what he was warning about. Thinking about Gramps makes me cry coz he will be missing me so bad. Why did stupid Ma bring me to this place he worked so hard to get us away from?

The streets get cleaner as we walk, less junk. People dressed in nice clothes, going places, not sitting around. We pass shops, and the Ape stops to buy a fizzy drink with money from Ma's tin. That's not what Ma's money is for. It's special money for doctors or medicine or food in the middle of winter when there's nothing left to scavenge or trade and the garden's gone slow. It's for family and friends. Not mean people.

Ma takes a sip like it don't matter and offers the can to me. I shake my head, and frown at her like I'm the ma and she's a bad kid who's wasted good money. Half of Ma's hard-earned tin's already wasted on that fat-headed man for his stupid car, when I would've sooner seen the Ape beat up and left in the gutter.

The Ape snatches the can back and sucks at it and screws up his face and cups his fat lip in his other hand for a moment. I'm glad his lip hurts. I'm glad Fat Head took the car back. Now when I run to the farm I know he won't be coming after me in that stupid car. I won't have to hear the scary whipping grass in the wide yellow sea.

We walk again for a long time, Ma white-knuckled dragging me, toe-stubbing along the concrete footpaths, till the houses get huge and gardens of flowers and hedges stretch out before us, and it takes thirty dragging steps to get past each one.

"Get on my back. I'll carry you," the Ape says to me and turns around like I'm gonna just jump up there.

"I'd rather eat a bucket of compost," I tell him and keep walking.

"Cha!" Ma growls.

"She shouldn't talk to me like that!" the Ape says.

"We're all tired, Danny," Ma says and leads me on.

After a couple more streets, she turns down a laneway and stops at a side gate. She turns back to the Ape. "I'll probably have Wednesday off," she says, like she ain't gonna see him till then. Finally something good's happening. He's gonna leave.

He nods. "Make her mind her manners, or they'll sack her and we'll be stuck with another mouth to feed," he says and gives Ma a kiss on her cheek.

"Give Ma her tin back," I tell him.

He screws up his nose and one side of his top lip and turns away.

I run around in front of him, make him stop. "It's hers and you need to give it back to her."

"Peony, no," Ma says reaching for me. "We're a family now. We share the money."

"Then he won't mind you looking after it," I say, ducking under her arm and staying put. "You worked hard for it. You should hold on to it."

The Ape man smiles down at me. "Your ma trusts me," he says.

"Don't you trust her? She don't give money to people who blap her in the face, or spend it on stupid drinks," I say.

The Ape screws up his eyes at me.

"It'll probably be safer here," Ma says and shrugs like she don't even care.

The Ape reaches inside his jacket and pulls out the tin and pushes it into Ma's hands. Then he turns and strides off up the laneway.

Ma grabs my shoulders and turns me to face her and runs her fingers through my hair and straightens my clothes. "Why you wanna go making him mad all the time?" she asks, and doesn't even wait for an answer, but I'm not gonna anyway, coz I'm still mad. "We gonna work here, together, me and you, and when we got enough money, we're gonna move to a place of our own. So you got to work hard. You got to show your best manners," she says and gives up trying to get my hair to behave. She wraps her long skinny fingers around my wrist again and stabs at a number panel on the gate with her other hand. The gate beeps and unlatches.

The house behind that big ol' gate is maybe ten times the size of Foreman's. It's all made of red bricks and some of the windows are bigger than our whole shed. The windows are staring down at me, making me feel like the smallest pest to ever set foot in that garden.

"Cha!" I breathe and dig my heels into the soft green lawn as Ma drags me across it. We don't belong here. Someone's gonna chase us off at any moment.

"Peony!" Ma says and jerks me forwards. She pulls me around the back of the house, up some steps and into a big kitchen. The white tiles are cold and smooth on my bare feet. A fat lady stands with a hunk of bloody meat on a bench in front of her and a pile of string in her hand.

A PROMISE
IS A PROMISE

"Rosie!" the fat lady says like she's telling Ma off. "Where you been? I'm run off my feet trying to keep up with everything upstairs and down!"

"Sorry," Ma says and jerks her head at me. "We ran into a problem."

"This is your daughter?" she asks. "Why's she all banged up?"

Ma nods. "Jumped out the window of the car." She lowers her head towards me. "Peony, say hello to Ivy." She pushes me in the middle of my back like I'm supposed to know how to say hello in proper manners.

I step up and hold out my hand like I seen Foreman

and Gramps do on the farm. "How ya going, Ivy?" I say.

Ivy holds her hands up to show her bloody palms and I drop my handshake hand.

"She's never gonna pass for fourteen, Rosie. What're you thinking?" Ivy says.

"She's strong and she's smart," Ma says.

"And she's dirty," Ivy says, and points at my feet spilling dust on her white tiles, toes manky with dried blood.

Ma sighs. She drags me through a door at the side of the kitchen. It's full of big white machines and piles of folded clothes. In one corner is a small bed, made up nicely with white sheets, and in the other corner behind half a wall is a toilet. There's a door at the back to another room.

"Why's she tying that dead thing down?" I whisper, looking back past Ma to Ivy grunting as she wraps the meat in string and ties it off.

"Shh!" Ma says.

There's a big silver basin next to the white machines, and Ma shoves a plug in and fills it. Steam rises and I lean over the sink and swish my fingers around. It's warm. Warm straight out of the wall. I open the cupboard below the basin, expecting to see a little fire going in there to heat the water, but no, it's just full of bright-colored bottles and buckets and rags.

"Peony, don't go poking around in stuff," Ma says and shuts the cupboard. "Get your clothes off and get in that sink."

"What?" I say.

She drops one eyebrow. "You heard."

I peel out of my shorts and my undies and my T-shirt, stand on the stool and swing one leg up and into the water. It burns and stings my toes, but before I can pull it out again, Ma's hoisting my arse up and dumping me into the sink.

I sit there, with my knees up by my chin as she scrubs my skin with a rough brush and soaps up my face and hair, and washes everything out again. Slowly the stinging of each little graze dies with the heat of the water. She scrubs each of my feet so hard they start bleeding again and when she lifts me out to stand on the cold white tiles I watch the blood make streaks and swirls in the puddles dripping from my body.

"Dry yourself," Ma orders and wraps a fluffy blue towel around me. She hurries to the bed and slides a cardboard box out from under it. On top are some nicely folded clothes that I've seen her wear, and under that is

66

my best clothes from when I left her getting on the bus and streaked across the field back to Gramps. Back to Gramps, promising him I'd never leave again. I suck in a deep breath, coz a promise is a promise, and crying like a toddler won't get my promise done.

CLUMSY SHOE FEET

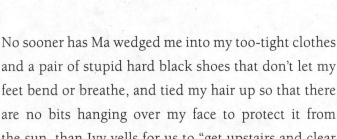

No sooner has Ma wedged me into my too-tight clothes and a pair of stupid hard black shoes that don't let my feet bend or breathe, and tied my hair up so that there are no bits hanging over my face to protect it from the sun, than Ivy yells for us to "get upstairs and clear away her ladyship's lunch things while she's having her piano lessons."

I'm stomping into my shoes so hard as Ma drags me from the kitchen that I get a fright to find I'm stomping on wood so polished and shiny I can see up my own trouser legs. When I lift my head, I'm in a room as big as a packing shed. But this ain't no packing shed. It's got floor rugs with crazy patterns I've never seen before, and huge furniture, so huge I reckon I could sleep on one of the chairs really well, but my feet wouldn't even touch the floor if I sat on them. There's benches made of shiny wood with curly feet and carved decorations, and on top of them are big glasses with flowers sticking out and silver framed pictures of a family. Either side of the window hang curtains, but not just curtains for covering the window. These curtains hang from the ceiling to the floor and look as heavy as wet blankets, heavy as the waterfall when Foreman opens the sluice to water the trees.

Ma jerks me along over the rug to the bottom of the stairs. I dance my clumsy shoe feet so I don't step on the winding bits of pattern that look like flowers. The railing on the stair is made of wood and curves away at the bottom like a gnarly tree caught in the wind for a thousand years, but polished and shiny. "Come on, Peony!" Ma grumbles and pulls me so my hand doesn't get to follow the winding of the railing. I stumble up the stairs after her.

At the top of the stairs is a hallway so wide a fruit truck could drive down it. It's got more of the patterned rugs and I want to just stand still and check out the patterns for a while, and the patterns on the ceilings and the fancy lights, but Ma drags me to a table on one side of the hall and picks up a tray there and shoves it into my hands. Somewhere up the hallway, music plays and stops and plays again.

"All the people who live in this building must be super-cherries," I say.

"Ha. All," Ma mutters. "Just one family."

I look down at all the doors in the hallway. They must have a lot of children and cousins and aunties and grans and gramps living in this family. And maybe babies like Mangojoy. I like MJ. If they have babies, I know how to make them laugh. I'll take care of the babies and the family will like me and I'll tell them about Mangojoy and how AJ and I look after him heaps, coz his mum's not well, and then maybe they'll take me home, coz they'll understand how important it is to everyone that I stay and work on the farm.

Ma points to a huge shiny wood door in front of me. "Go in that room. Go to the table in there and collect all the plates, whether they're dirty, clean or still got food on 'em, and put them on the tray and carry the tray back down to Ivy. Do you think you can do that without breaking any?"

"Cha! I carry packing trays all the time," I remind her, and somehow I've agreed to work with her without even saying so. But I guess I gotta play along till I can get home to Gramps.

She nods and pushes the handle on the door so it glides open and then she heads off up the hall leaving me to it.

I push the door open a little more and peer in. It's a huge room. A whole family must live in here coz there's a bed and a couch and a table set up under the window. There's also a TV and some kind of games, lying on the floor. I tiptoe around the games to the table and put the tray down on the chair. I can't believe that there's a biscuit with a bit of jam left on the table with just one bite out of it and also half a glass of some yellowish water. I sniff it. Apples! It's apple juice! I look back at the door, pick up the glass and drink it all. So sweet. So fruity. I wish I could tell Applejoy about this. About me actually tasting apple juice like a super-cherry Urb! I shove the biscuit into my mouth too. Apricot jam, just like Gramps's apricot slices but sweeter, and more bitter too, coz apricot is our special treat, and here, even when it's been made into sweet jam, someone just bites an apricot biscuit and dumps it like it's not a special thing at all. I empty all the plates off the

71

table onto the tray, heft it up and carry it carefully back across the room, chewing my apricot jam as long as I can, so I can keep the taste of home on my tongue.

I get back out the door to the top of the stairs and move the tray out of the way so I can see my clumsy shoes on the steps. If I had bare feet, I'd be able to feel the edge of the steps. This is stupid. If I can run along branches in bare feet and not fall, then I can get this tray down the stairs in bare feet a lot safer. I kick my shoes off, leave them lying at the top of the stairs, and carry the tray to the bottom, feeling the way in my new white socks, with blood already leaked into the fabric from my stubbed toes.

At the bottom of the stairs I put the tray on the floor and run back up to grab my shoes. But when I get four steps from the top, a girl about my age is standing over them with her hands on her hips.

THE BEETLE-HAIRED
GIRL

"Who are you?" she shouts down at me like I shouldn't even be here.

"Who are you?" I shout back up her. I don't reckon she's even my age yet. She's just got bigger bones, like she's been eating soft oat bun with pig meat on it her whole life. Her hair is long and black and shines like a beetle's back, ripples like tap water when she shakes her head. She sticks her chin up so high I can see right up her nose.

"I am Esmeralda Pasquale and THIS," she waves her hand around and plonks it back on her hip, "is my house! I don't like people leaving their old ugly shoes at the top of the stairs to trip me over!"

73

"Well, I am Peony, and those are not old ugly shoes, they're new ugly shoes. Ugly like your scritchy voice!" I say and put my hands on my hips too. And though I'm four steps down, we're having a face-off. She don't get to diz me coz I have to wear stupid shoes that won't let my feet feel the steps.

Esmawhatserface pulls her foot back and boots my new ugly shoes, sending them bouncing on down the stairs, just as Ma appears at the top of the stairs next to her. One shoe stops halfway down, but the other carries on and clatters into the tray at the bottom of the stairs sending spoons and plates skittering across the floor.

"Peony!" Ma says like I'm the one who did it.

I open my mouth to say something but already Ma has her hand on Esmathingy's shoulder and she's saying softly, "I'm so sorry, gorgeous flower. You're quite right. It's dangerous to leave things at the top of the stairs."

I've never heard Ma use the word "quite" before. Sounds fancy. What's it mean? A little bit? She's a little bit right? Still, woulda been no problem if stupid-head just stepped over them, and didn't kick them down the stairs.

Ma turns to me. "Peony, don't you have something to say to Esmeralda?"

I look at Ma for a clue. I don't know how she thinks I know manners and stuff.

"Something nice," Ma says.

"Oh," I mumble. Then I smile. "She's quite good at ending a face-off."

Ma grabs me and drags me sock-slipping down the stairs. She shoves me at my shoe halfway down and I grab it, and at the bottom she sits me on the step and tells me to put my shoes on, while she gathers the plates and spoons back onto the tray.

"If anything's broken, it's her fault," I whisper. "She kicked the shoes."

"Should'a been On. Your. Feet," Ma says, banging out the last three words like I don't know how to wear shoes.

"I was trying to carry the tray," I explain, but already Ma has scooped up the tray and is heading back to the kitchen. I pull on my second shoe and twist to look up the stairs. The girl is leaning over the railing staring at me, her hair flowing down the shiny rail like it wants to trickle all the way to the bottom. She sticks her tongue out.

I hold up my rude finger and follow Ma to the kitchen.

THE DELICATE FLOWER

The soft white bread is full of air and flattens on the roof of my mouth. Ivy smeared it with yellow that melts on my warm tongue, and fills my mouth with sunshine. Greasy, yummy sunshine.

Ivy sat me on a stool at the bench and gave me this while she talks at me.

"Miss Esmeralda is very sensitive," she says.

I swallow. "What's this called?" I wave the slice of bread at her.

"You never had a bread and butter sandwich before?" she asks, and looks at Ma for a moment. "Anyway, you have to treat Miss Esmeralda with care, she's a delicate flower."

"Din't look so delicate when she was booting my shoes down the stairs," I point out.

"Nevertheless," Ivy says in a way that means "stop talking and listen to me." "You had best mind your manners when you speak to Esmeralda or any of the Pasquales. That means saying "please" and "thank you" and "so nice to meet you" and all the rest."

"I don't know all the rest." I yawn so big a bit of bread and butter falls out of my mouth and I have to pick it up off the bench to eat it again.

"Then you best learn. Quick smart," Ivy says and waggles a finger in my face.

"Yes, Boz," I say, coz she looks a bit like Foreman, the way her eyebrows are fuzzy like big caterpillars on a branch.

Ivy shakes her head at me. "You got bags I could pack for a holiday under your eyes. Your mother dragging you around the countryside. Go to bed for a while before the Pasquales get home so you'll look half decent when you meet them," she tells me.

Ma waves me through to the small bed next to the big white machines humming and slushing to themselves. "We sleep here," she says and points at the small bed. She sits me down on the bed and takes my shoes off like I'm just a little kid.

77

"I don't like it here," I tell her.

"Well, we all have to learn to do things we don't like or we'll never get ahead," she says and lifts my legs onto the bed.

"I don't want to get ahead. I want to go home," I tell her.

"Shh, you're just tired. You'll feel better after a sleep," she says, like sleeping could change my mind about missing Gramps and Mags and AJ.

"If the Pasquales don't like me, can I go home?" I ask.

Ma drops her head and her dark eyes find mine. She holds out her cracked pointer finger with the chipped fingernail, and stabs it towards my nose. "If you do anything! Anything at all to make the Pasquales dislike you, I'll give you to that old lady in the street and she'll sell you for soup bones." Ma whispers it real low so I know she's serious.

SOUP BONES

Plates are clattering and a woman I don't know is shouting in the kitchen when I wake. I sit up, pull on my stupid shoes and tiptoe to the doorway. The kitchen is steamy and yummy warm-bread smelling.

A tiny woman with long black hair is clip-clopping about on tall heels. Her skin is smooth and her clothes look like they were stitched on her, they fit so perfectly. Giant black lashes flap on her eyelids as she bosses Ivy and Ma about the kitchen.

"Make sure the oil is hot, hot, hot. I want crisp!" she says to Ivy.

"Yes, Ma'am!" Ivy says.

Somewhere behind the door to the rest of the house a bell is dinging, then stopping, then dinging again.

"And three chillis. Not one. I could hardly taste it last time," the woman says, and she clops to the cupboard and hauls it open. "Where's the tea? Not the black one, the other one. You know the one."

The dinging sounds again, goes on longer this time.

Ivy hovers over her shoulder. "Yes, Ma'am. There, in the blue tin."

The woman grabs it, spins on her heel and plops the tin on the benchtop in front of Ma. "Rosie, make us a pot of this, three cups."

"Yes, Ma'am!" Ma says.

"Rosie! Can't you hear Mr. Pasquale's bell? Hop to it!" the woman snaps.

Ma runs through the door.

"What is wrong with her lately?" the woman asks Ivy.

"She's just tired," Ivy says.

The woman snorts. "From what, I don't know," she mutters, then her long black lashes flap up, and two green eyes look right at me.

I think maybe I can duck back behind the doorframe but Ivy turns and says, "Peony, get out here!"

I take two steps into the kitchen.

"This is her daughter?" the woman asks Ivy like I'm not even here.

Ivy nods.

"Are you fourteen, Peony?" the woman asks.

"Yes, Ma'am," I say coz that's what everyone else has been saying. Then I add, "Almost."

"Well, how old are you?" she asks.

"Twelve?" I try.

The woman, who must be Mrs. Pasquale, turns to Ivy. "She's very small for twelve."

"Yes, Ma'am," Ivy says and gives me a look with one fluffy caterpillar hunching on her brow.

"Has she met Esmeralda?" Mrs. Pasquale asks.

"Yes, Ma'am," Ivy says again and gives me another hunched caterpillar brow.

"Tell me, Peony," Mrs. Pasquale asks. "Did Esmeralda like you?"

"Yes, Ma'am," I say again. "But that's for her to say."

Mrs. Pasquale laughs. "Well, come on, let's find out." She walks to the door and holds it.

"Go on then," Ivy says and prods me towards the door with one fat finger in my back.

I step through and Mrs. Pasquale clip-clops ahead, over the patterned rug, past the staircase, to a table where

81

Esmeralda sits with a man. The man is fussing about his knives and forks like they're special. Laying them out and bossing at Ma to put them in some kind of order.

He slams down a spoon and Ma jumps. "It's not that hard!" he barks.

I step forward, coz if some Urb is gonna blap Ma across the face, then I'll be blapping him right back. I don't care that he's bigger than me, or if me and Mags already blapped Ma ourselves months ago. Ma is family, and you gotta stick up for family.

The man looks at me. His hair is real short and smoothed back so shiny I think it might not be hair at all but maybe some kind of hat.

"This is Peony, Rosie's girl," Mrs. Pasquale says.

"Hello, Peony," Mr. Pasquale says, and Ma gives me a side-eye like she can't even watch what kind of mistakes I'm about to make or the smacking I'm about to get, and takes off back to the kitchen.

"Hello," I say slow and careful. Can I do things wrong if I'm slow and careful? I'll treat them Pasquales like the most delicate blossoms.

"And you've already met Esmeralda, I hear," Mrs. Pasquale says. "Esmeralda, dear, do you like our newest member of staff?"

Esmeralda turns to me and smiles, and I'm soup bones. I'm out on the street in rags starving and sold for soup bones. I shoulda never done the face-off. Should never have done the rude finger. Esmeralda opens her mouth to say the words that will turn me to soup.

"She's quite nice," Esmeralda says. But under the table, low, so no one tall can see, she holds up her rude finger.

MY GRANDMOTHER'S NAME

I knock on the polished wooden door. The sun went down hours ago and at home I'd already be in bed, listening to the sound of bats and nightbirds. But Ivy slapped the back of my head when I fell asleep standing at the bench, and told me to get upstairs to collect Esmeralda's dirty clothes for washing. I'm beginning to see why Ma's like she is when she comes home.

"Yes?" Esmeralda's voice is tiny behind the door.

"Ivy sent me for your washing," I say.

"Come in," Esmeralda says.

I push the door open and go in. Esmeralda is sitting on a chair wearing fluffy flowery pants and matching top, jabbing at something in her hand and pointing it at the TV. The TV makes stupid blips and beeps and Esmeralda groans and turns to me like I did something wrong. "Well?" she says.

"Your washing," I say. "Ivy sent me."

Esmeralda rolls her eyes like I'm stupid. "The bathroom." She jabs a finger at a door past the bed. Her parents aren't in the bed and I don't know where they vanished to after eating. Maybe Esmeralda is too noisy for them to sleep so they're sitting out somewhere near a fire chatting till she goes to bed. I miss Gramps's ol' growly voice talking low and quiet outside our shed at night.

I go to the door and push it open. It's a whole other room, all covered in white tiles like the kitchen floor and there's a giant bathtub like maybe a queen would have, as well as a tiny sink and a toilet. There's a basket in the corner, but there are towels and the clothes that Esmeralda wore earlier draped over the edge of the basket and all around the floor. I pick up all the clothes and the wet towels and bundle them up and head back into the other room. Esmeralda is stabbing at the thing in her hand and strange blobby creatures are leaping around the TV, beeping and bopping again. I stop and try to figure out what she's doing, and she throws her arms up in the

85

air and turns around to frown at me like I did something wrong again.

"What now?" she asks.

"Where's your ma?" I ask.

"In their room," she snaps.

"They don't share this room?" I ask.

"Are you stupid?" she says.

"Stomp you," I mumble. "Where's the rest of your family, like your cousins and grandpas?" I try.

"They live in their own houses," she says.

"Cha! This whole big house is for just three people?" I ask, they must share that huge bathroom though. Twenty-something families share one bathroom down on the farm. It's just a tin shed that don't go all the way to the ground with a concrete floor and a toilet. We wash ourselves using tin buckets that we put on the edge of the fire in winter to warm up. No fancy hot water taps for us.

"Do you have any more stupid questions?" Esmeralda asks.

"Yes," I say. "What are you wearing and what kind of weird name is Esmeralda?"

Esmeralda throws the thing in her hand down on the chair and stretches up to her full height. "It is my

GRANDMOTHER'S NAME!" she bellows, like that's all super-cherries.

"She ain't using it no more?" I ask.

Esmeralda sucks her top lip behind her bottom teeth, rips out her rude finger and stabs it towards me.

"Cha," I mutter and leave the room.

BURGLARS AND
BAD PEOPLE

Ivy meets me back in the kitchen with an even bigger bundle of clothes and we stuff them all into the front of one of the big white machines. Ma is already stretched out on the tiny bed snoring softly.

"Hope we're not keeping you up," Ivy calls to her, but Ma don't stir. Ivy puts smelly blue liquid into the machine and shuts it and flicks a few buttons on the front. She looks at me watching her. "It's a washing machine. It washes clothes. Don't you know nuthin', girl?"

"I can practically run a whole fruit farm," I say.

"Fat lotta good that'll do you here," Ivy points out, then she brushes her teeth, and sits on the loo. "Get ready for bed, girl!" she tells me as she wipes her bits and flushes, then she flicks out the light in the kitchen and goes through the door at the back of the room. She has a bed in there and a chest of drawers. The door shuts with a click and I'm alone. Now I can go back to the farm.

I open the back door and slide out into the cool night garden and go around to the side gate, but it's locked up tight. The number buttons glow, promising me they'll let me out if I can guess the right ones. I poke four of them in the shape I think I remember Ma doing this morning but nothing happens. I try again and try again, each number beeping out into the dark, trying to wake up all the Pasquales and Ma and Ivy and get me caught.

I kick off my stupid shoes and peel off my blood-toe-sticking socks and climb the brick wall instead. Digging my sore toes into the cracks between the bricks, and hanging on to a tiny tree until I'm on my stomach on top of the wall, trying to haul the rest of me up.

"Where are you going?" Esmeralda whispers.

"Home," I whisper back, and sit up on the wall. She has a window open and she's leaning out, and her eyes are round, reflecting the lights from the street.

"You can't go out there alone!" she whispers.

"Cha," I say. "I ain't afraid of the dark."

"Nor am I. It's the bad people in the dark that will grab you and hurt you and do terrible things to you," she whispers.

"What people?" I ask. "The raggy people? They're just hungry."

"There's worse than that out there," she warns. "And children can't go anywhere alone, don't you know anything?"

"I go places alone on the farm all the time," I say. "Anyway, it's so dark and I'm quiet, they won't see me at all."

"You could run all through the night and when the sun comes up, you'll still be in the city and then the bad people will grab you."

I swing my legs about to jump off the wall anyway. Far away in the night there's a bang and some shouting.

"That's the guards chasing off the burglars," Esmeralda whispers and she pulls the window in towards her like she's worried burglars will be coming in through it any minute. "They come every night, almost. Come to take stuff to sell. They'll take you too if they can. Or if you just stand too close to the window, they might shoot you dead."

"Cha!" I say, and lean forwards to check the jump to the street.

Esmeralda gasps, and then sobs behind me. "Please! Don't!" she says, like it's her that's gonna face the burglars and bad people.

I turn back and study the side of her face lit from the streetlight. "What do you care? You's just all shouty and rude at me."

"I'm not!" she says.

"You's all this," I put my hands on my hips and dip my head from side to side and whisper, "Wa, wa, wa. And this!" I show her my rude finger.

"What's that even mean?" she asks.

I snort. Then I laugh. I laugh till tears run down my cheeks and I wipe them away.

Esmeralda laughs too.

"It's rude," I say. "It's the rudest thing you can ever do!"

"Really?" she says. "The rudest?"

I laugh again. "Is that why you told your ma I was nice? Coz you didn't know how rude I was?"

Esmeralda shrugs. "I was bored. I thought you might be fun for a while," she says like she thinks maybe people are toys.

"You's weird. I gotta get back to the farm. Gramps and Mags miss me, and if any bees get hurt, Foreman's gonna call me to replace them for sure."

91

"You were a bee?" she asks. "We studied the bees at school and we took a bus trip out to see the bees working."

"I'm almost a bee. I'm gonna bee soon. Real soon," I say. "That's why I gotta get back. They need me. I'm gonna be a bee soon, and one day I'll be a Foreman."

Esmeralda nods like she finally understands. "You can't get back by just climbing over a wall and running through the city," she says. "You have to know the way. I'll let you back into the house."

Last place I wanna go is back in the house. But I think maybe Esmeralda has a plan and maybe she knows a reason why I can't get home just by running.

She closes the window and a little while later a light spills out from the kitchen window. I jump down off the wall and go around to the back door. The grass is soft and cool on my feet.

CREEK ROAD

The back door cracks open and Esmeralda's head pokes out. "Peony!" she whispers and waves me in.

I sit on a stool at the kitchen bench while she opens the fridge and pulls out cans of drink and opens one for each of us. I never had a drink from a can before. Bubbles tickle my nose whenever I go to drink from the hole, but when I finally take a sip, it is so sweet it carves a cold sticky channel down my throat. I cough and put the can down.

"What's your address?" she asks.

"My address?"

"Yeah, what's the number and name of the road?

You have to put that information into your nav so you can find your way," she says.

"My nav?" I ask.

"Well, you don't have a phone because you're poor, but other people who drive cars and taxis do."

"Cha! I'm not going home in a car or a taxi," I say.

"Yes, but you need a phone and an address so you don't get lost," she says.

"Do you have a phone?" I ask.

"Yes," she says.

"Can you give it to me?"

"Maybe," she says slowly. "Do you have an address?"

I shake my head.

"What's the name of the street you live on?" she asks.

I try to remember the sign near the bus stop, but our lessons are over loudspeaker and I'm not good at reading. "Creek Road," I say finally but there's a word in front of creek I can't remember. "Something Creek Road."

Esmeralda flicks her long hair behind her ear and goes to a screen in the wall. She pokes a button and it lights up. I follow her over there as she taps out the letters that make the word "creek" just like the street sign. She's clever. She'll have me home real quick with all these super-cherry devices.

She groans and turns to me. "There's like fifty million Creek Roads in this state," she says.

"But which one has a fruit farm on it?" I ask.

"I don't know!" she snaps like I've said something stupid. "You'll have to ask your mother for the exact address."

"I'm running away, remember?" I say.

"Oh yeah," she says. Then she clicks some other buttons and the screen does some beeping and strange little creatures chase her finger across the screen. "This one's fun!" she says.

I put my hands on my hips and step back. "Are you gonna help me or not?" I say.

"Tomorrow," she says and punches the button on the screen to turn it off. "I'm too tired now and we need an address. I'm going to bed."

Then she's gone through the kitchen door, leaving me alone with two half-drunk cans of bubbly drink. I put them in the fridge, flick off the kitchen light, feel my way into the the room where the washing machine slushes and rumbles, and use Ivy's toothbrush before I crawl under the blanket and wriggle my back up against Ma's feet.

BURNING HOT

It's still dark when Ivy jerks my ear. "On your feet, lazy bones!"

I slap away her pinching fingers and pull the blanket over my head.

"The Pasquales need breakfast, hop to it!" Ivy shouts.

"Blossom," Ma groans at me like we're friends again.

I sit up and rub the fuzz from my eyes. Ma's sitting on the bed hunched over a bowl, heaving air and drool.

"You sick?" I ask.

Ma takes a deep breath. "It's the baby. Must be another girl. I was like this with you and Magnolia."

"The baby makes you sick?" I ask.

96

She holds the small mound of her stomach in one hand and nods. "Please help Ivy in the kitchen. I can't even smell food in the morning."

I breathe out and screw my lips to the side so she knows I'm not happy about my new life. But I get up, use the toilet and then go find a cloth, rinse it under the cold tap at the sink and lay it on her forehead.

Ma smiles, then she looks at my feet and all around on the floor. "Blossom, where are your shoes and socks?"

"I left them at the back door," I say.

Ma nods. "In rich folks' houses they expect you to keep your feet covered and your shoes perfectly clean."

"Cha!" I say, like I'm annoyed at all the rules, and hurry through to the kitchen. I throw open the back door and run out.

"Peony! The flies!" Ivy yells after me as I duck around the side of the house and find my shoes and socks in the bushes. I'm back sitting on the doorstep, pulling on my socks by the time she gets her head out the door.

"Come on. Stop mucking about," she says.

She makes me cart food and plates and knives and forks from the kitchen to the table, then comes out and rearranges them like the Pasquales don't even have their own arms to reach for things.

Then I'm back to the kitchen to stand over the hot pan as pink bits of pig fry and spit under my nose and I turn them over with a pair of tongs. I've never tasted pink meat before so I pick up a bit and give it a lick. My tongue burns.

"Rosie! Rosie!"

I drop the meat back in the pan. Mrs. Pasquale's heels click across the floor outside the kitchen door and she bursts in.

"Peony, get me the Greek yogurt, put it in the black jug, the tall one, you know the one," she says, as I lick pig grease from my lips.

"Yes, Ma'am," I say, but I don't know about black jugs or Greek thingies, so I stand there, like the stupidest new pest who don't even know where to find a caterpillar or how to sharpen their bit of fence wire to stab the beetles through the back. I stand there with my face burning. I burn hot at Ma for bringing me here to a place I can't fit in. Hot at Mrs. Pasquale for being so bossy. Hot at Esmeralda for not helping me properly last night when I had a chance to leave.

"Peony! Now!" Mrs. Pasquale claps her hands at me like I'm a naughty chook, so I turn away and open the nearest cupboard, even though I'm not supposed to

98

go poking around in stuff. The cupboard is full of pots.

"Gah!" Mrs. Pasquale turns and trit-trots back out to the other room. "Ivy!" she screams.

Ivy bustles back in, big hips jiggling, boobs heaving up and down, and I duck around behind the kitchen bench so she can't thwack me around the head. "Burning the bacon, standing round like a lump, what good are you?" she asks.

I quick-fill my mind with all the good things I can do on the farm. All the pests I know how to catch, that time Foreman called, "Good bee," how fast I can run, Gramps's hugs, how I can always make Mangojoy giggle and AJ smile his most excellent smile. One eye waters up.

Ivy scrapes out the pink pig meat onto a plate and shoves it at me. "Get that through to Mr. Pasquale!"

I take it and carry it out and put it on the table in front of Mr. Pasquale.

He don't say anything about it, just keeps on talking to Mrs. Pasquale. I head back to the kitchen. Esmeralda is on the stairs, her beetle-black hair shimmering as she bounces down, step to step. She smiles at me, and I sniff my nose high in the air and carry on. But back in the kitchen, Ivy shoves a tall black jug at me full of sour white thick stuff.

"Take this out to the table," she says.

I take it from her and stomp back to the door. Then I stop and take some deep breaths, coz now I'm burning hot at the whole world and I want to throw this sour white stuff at the next person who looks at me.

"Peony?" Ma whispers.

She's standing at the door to the little room beside the kitchen, hanging on to the doorframe and looking at me with her eyes full of worry. Probably just from throwing up so much. She don't care about me.

I take the stupid jug of stupid stuff to the table, I don't look at no one, and I get back to the kitchen, without looking at no one, and I go out the back door to the garden.

"The flies!" Ivy yells after me through the open back door.

WE ARE BETTER THAN A TEAM

I go out into the back garden and find the thickest bush and crawl into the cold shadow underneath it. The cold is nice on my hot face.

The back door clicks shut and Ma's black rubber shoes scuff down the steps and across the grass and stop next to the bush. She drops down on her hands and knees. She has on big purple rubber gloves, like the packing ladies wear when they clean off the packing tables at the end of the day.

"Blossom," she says. "What's wrong?"

"I don't like it here," I say. "There's nuthin' I can do right."

"You're smart. You'll pick it up," Ma says.

"I'm already smart about farm things. I know what I have to do, and I work hard, and nobody bosses me round or looks at me like I'm stupid," I say and wrap my arms around my knees.

"But here you earn cold hard cash, and the Pasquales don't mean to be bossy. They just like things how they like things," Ma says. "Come have some breakfast and help me wash the dishes." She waves a purple glove at me.

I shake my head. "It's not even important. Esmeralda can pick up her own clothes. Mr. Pasquale can put his own knives and forks on the table. Back home, if me and Mags don't do our job the trees suffer, the fruit suffers. What we do is important."

"You, me and Ivy," Ma says, "we're a team. We're the team that keeps the Pasquales going, keeps their house clean, their food cooked and their child cared for."

I crawl out and look into Ma's dark eyes. I take her purple glove in my hand. "They don't care about you, Ma. They don't care that you're sick every morning, just that someone brings them their stupid fried pink pig meat. Come home. You got a bit of money to get some medicine if you need it. Come home to our shed and have the baby and let me and Mags and Gramps look after you for a while. We are better than a team. We are a family." I peel off her purple glove and turn over her worn wrinkled hand, rest it in mine, run my fingers over her short and splitting nails.

"And after that? After we get through a couple of winters and there's five mouths to feed and no money left?" Ma asks.

"I'll be a bee, and Mags will be in charge of pests or have a better job—"

"And Danny? What about Danny? We're going to have this baby together, and he can't live at the orchard. He's only ever lived in real houses before." Ma pulls her hand out of mine and looks across the yard as if she's looking at a different world to the one she's sitting in.

"The Ape? He's gonna take your money for himself."

"Peony! You don't know nuthin'. You're too young to understand," she says.

"He hit me, Ma. He hit you. He's gonna hit you again and he's gonna hit the baby and he—"

Ma stands up. "Peony!" She hurries back across the grass, then stops and turns back. "He's made a promise to change, to look after me and the baby, and I have to give him a chance."

I scowl at her coz she's just being stupid. She goes in the back door, then yells out, "Come get your breakfast or miss out!" and the door clicks shut.

So I go back in and sit at the bench and try the smelly white stuff and it's sour and weird and smells like the little room next to the kitchen did when Ma was vomiting. I don't get so much to eat coz we're sharing the stuff on the bench and Ivy knocks it back like a starving cocky. She knocks back one of the opened cans of bubbly drink from the fridge, which I could only sip at coz it was too fizzy and too sweet.

"Get upstairs and tell Miss Esmeralda her car will be here in ten minutes," Ivy says to me between noisy sucks at the second can.

I don't say nothing, just get up and leave Ma and Ivy to it and stomp up the stairs to Esmeralda's room.

Even before I can touch the door she's yelling, "Go away!"

"Shut up!" I yell back.

SLIDE LIKE
TRACTOR OIL

A little while later the door opens a crack, and Esmeralda's eye peeks at me. "What?" she says.

"Ivy said something about a car in ten minutes," I say.

Esmeralda lets the door drift open. "Can you get my boots from the wardrobe? The red ones."

"No," I say.

Esmeralda frowns. "You have to do what I tell you."

"Make me," I say.

"Go get Rosie, she always helps me dress, and she likes to plait my hair," Esmeralda says and I tilt my head and make my face smooth and hard as a packing crate, coz my ma never helps me dress. She never did anything special with Mags's or my hair, but here she is doing it for a girl who's not even family.

"She says I have the prettiest hair in the world." Esmeralda shakes her head, making her hair slide like tractor oil, and smiles as if maybe she knows she's getting to me, even though I'm standing here wearing my hardest packing crate face.

So I change it. I put on my super-cherry smile and stomp over to the door that's half open, and inside is full of clothes hanging in rows, and racks of shoes. I grab the red boots, carry them back to Esmeralda.

"Is this why you stopped me from leaving last night?" I whisper it low, the way Ma does when she's mad at me. "So I could run and fetch you all the things you's too lazy to get yourself?"

"I'm not lazy!" she says.

I pull myself up taller than her and point my finger in her face. "Don't you get in my way ever. You'll be sorry." I throw the boots at her feet, which makes her jump, then I super-cherry smile for real and leave the room.

I'm at the top of the stairs when she calls out, "Peony!" And it's tiny and echoey, like a bat in the night.

I stop. But I don't turn back.

She tiptoes across the rug behind me. "I stopped you

106

because I'm afraid to go outside. When I saw you going over the wall, I couldn't stop shaking. But also, I thought you could help make me not so afraid."

I still don't turn around; I just shrug. "Maybe I'll help you, before I go," I say and run down the stairs.

THAT BEAUTIFUL SIGN

Ma has me scrubbing the black off that stupid pan where the pig meat burned. Grease slicks my hands, so when Esmeralda starts up screaming from the other room I'm left wiping my hands on my shirtfront as I run.

Esmeralda is hanging on to the frame of the open front door while a man in a black hat tugs her hand.

I race over to kick him for trying to steal our Esmeralda, but when I get there, she's screaming, "No! Bring it closer."

"I can't, Miss," the man says. "It's as close as I can get it without ruining your mum's plants. Come on now, we'll be late."

Outside a car waits with its door open.

"Ez?" I ask.

She turns and looks at me and lets go of the frame and lunges at me instead. "Peony!" she says and wraps her hands around my arm. "You have to come with me. I can't go outside."

Ma runs up and pats Esmeralda's hair. "Blossom," she says, "it's alright. I'll hold your hand to the car."

So no flat-out dragging or toe-stubbing for Esmeralda. Is this even my ma?

"I want Peony to come with me. Peony isn't afraid," Esmeralda says.

"Peony can take you to the car too," Ma says.

"She has to come all the way to school. I hate going in the car alone," Esmeralda yells.

"But Blossom, we need Peony here to help clean the house," Ma says and a length of Esmeralda's shiny black hair slides through Ma's wrinkly-backed fingers. "And you have Jonagold with you all the way. You're never alone."

"Please!" Esmeralda says, winding her voice out long and high like a galah.

Ma turns her dark eyes on me and her serious face, and she drops her voice low. "You go with her, but you stay in the car, and then you come right back. Don't you give Jonagold any trouble. Don't you dare leave his side."

I nod. And Ma bundles me and Esmeralda out the front door, like we're one thing with four legs now, and into the back of the big car. She waves a finger at my face before she shuts the door on us.

Jonagold climbs in the front of the car, and the wide gates in front of us roll open. Esmeralda puts on her seat belt and waves at me to do the same. The car moves out onto the street and Esmeralda grabs my hand and squeezes.

The big houses fly past the window too fast for me to try and understand how huge they are, and how much wood and stone and bricks went into building these square-eyed monsters, and how many people might live in them. They can't all just have three people in each one.

"Ez?" I ask, but when I turn to her, her eyes are squeezed as tight as her fingers are wrapped around mine. "Open your eyes. There's nuthin' bad here."

She cracks one eye open and looks at me. "How come you call me Ez?" she says.

"Oh soz," I say. I'm s'posed to treat her like a cherry blossom, and I keep forgetting.

"No," she says and opens both eyes. "I like it. I don't

110

feel like scared little Esmeralda when you call me Ez. I feel brave, as if I could run along tree branches like a bee."

I laugh coz there's no way she could be a bee. She'd get to the first tree and tell me to do it for her.

Esmeralda screws up her face. "I could be a bee. My grandmother Esmeralda was a famous bee!"

"Really?" I ask.

"Yes, in the ballet," she says.

"Where's ballay?" I ask, but she just laughs.

"I'll show you when we get home." She leans forwards to Jonagold and says, "Take me to the factory."

"Miss Esmeralda, no. You're goin' straight to school," Jonagold says.

"It's on the way. I just want to show Peony, and you know it'll save time sitting in the drop-off queue if we're a little late." Esmeralda smiles at the side of Jonagold's head and he turns and glances at her and gives a nod.

Soon we're in some giant concrete park full of cars, next to a wide tin building built like a packing shed, but the size of about fifty packing sheds.

"My father owns this," Esmeralda says and waves a hand towards the giant white packing shed.

Jonagold drives the car in a loop and passes some

111

huge black glass windows in one end of the giant packing shed.

"My father's office is in there," she says and points at the windows. "In front of the coolstore."

I have no idea what a coolstore is, but on the front of those windows, lined up in a row, is a whole pile of signs. And one of the signs is the same as the sign on the packing boxes that we pack at my farm.

"That's my farm!" I yell and point at the sign. "The one with the green pear and two apricots on it!"

"Goulburn Valley Farms?" Esmeralda says.

It's a name I remember Foreman saying, so I nod and cling to the window as Jonagold drives the car back into the street.

Esmeralda slides across the seat a bit towards me as we drive away from that beautiful sign, my sign, my farm, Goulburn Valley Farms.

WALK LIKE A QUEEN

"Does your father own my farm?" I ask.

"No, he buys fruit from all those places in the signs," Esmeralda says. "He trucks the fruit back to the coolstore and stores it there till he sells it to people."

I sit back and think about this awhile. Esmeralda grabs my hand again in both hers. Outside the car, the city is getting busy. We are passing a lot of shops, and people are walking or driving slowly. Jonagold drives around a couple of stopped cars. The raggy people are here with their hands out and their sad tired faces.

"Jonagold, slow down at the fruit shop!" Esmeralda yells.

The car slows and Esmeralda unwraps her hand and points out the window. "My father owns that shop."

Glass squares fill the front window, lit up like they're under the strongest sunshine. Tiny balls of color are laid out on tissue paper and trays in each glass square. Pink and orange peaches sit in a row above a line of perfect deep purple plums, on top of another row of peaches, and another row of deep and dusty plums. They stripe their way down the tray. In another glass square, raspberry-red apples alternate with green apples and round oranges like they're having a contest to see who is brighter. Lemons dance in circles with green limes around a huge watermelon. The watermelon's green skin is full of lemon-colored streaks. Shiny mandarins are stacked up into a pyramid with bunches of wrinkled purple passionfruit. Blackberries, grapes, strawberries and raspberries sit in delicate heaps and call out to fingers to reach through the glass and take just one.

"Oh!" I say and my hand grabs at the car window. In the shop doorway sits a stack of packing cases. My packing cases. The end has a picture of a green pear and two apricots. Tiny orange apricots cover the top layer of the top box. Packed the way we pack them, tissue paper moulded up nicely around each one!

114

A truck is unloading boxes ahead of us, and when Jonagold drives around it, I see more of my farm's packing cases. I shake my hand out of Esmeralda's and grab for the door handle.

"I have to get in that truck!" I whisper to Esmeralda. "It can take me back to my farm when it goes to get more fruit!"

Esmeralda grabs my arm. "It's probably only going back to the coolstore," she says.

I shake her off and wrestle with the door again. It's locked. "You just want me to stay. But I can't. I'm needed at the farm," I say and look around for another way out.

"You sit tight, young Peony," Jonagold says. "Your mother will kill me if I come back without you."

Esmeralda cups her hand to my ear, leans in close. "We need a plan!" she whispers. "After school."

I look at her. "You promise?" I ask.

She nods.

The car pulls up to a big set of gates and a metal arm blocks our way. A man in a uniform with a gun walks around the car and Jonagold winds down the window on his side. "Jez," he says and nods at the guard.

"Morning, Jona," the guard says. "Dropping off one or two?"

My neck prickles, coz I can't go to school. I know my numbers but I hardly know all my letters and I can't read properly. I'll look stupid.

"Just Miss Esmeralda," Jonagold says, and I let my breath out.

The guard lifts the arm and the car rolls forwards up a driveway to a tall dark building. Lined up in front of it are lots of cars just like our one. Girls leap from the cars when they stop, slamming doors, and run, calling out hellos up to the entrance of the building. Esmeralda grips my hand tighter.

"Here, Miss Esmeralda?" Jonagold asks.

"No! Closer!" Esmeralda yells.

Jonagold waits for cars to pull away ahead and drives the car closer to the door. "Miss Esmeralda?" he asks again.

"Up there! Closer!" Esmeralda says.

"I can walk you," he says and sighs like he already knows she's not going to agree.

"Closer!" Esmeralda says.

The car in front doesn't move at all so Jonagold can't roll forwards anymore. He turns the car off and gets out and walks around to my door and opens it. "Miss Esmeralda, come on. It's only a short walk."

Esmeralda's hand in mine is slippery with sweat and

116

trembling. I guess I thought she was pretending to be scared, but she really is.

"Ez," I whisper. "You's brave like a bee."

Esmeralda looks at me and nods and swallows, and I slide across the seat towards Jonagold, who's waiting, holding the door, and get out. Esmeralda follows me as far as the car door but stops with just the toe of her shoe, and her hand in mine, outside the car.

I reach in and take her other hand off the seat. "You's a bee, Ez. You's the bravest thing in the world."

She looks up at me and her neck stretches up and her shoulders go back and her pointed toe reaches down for the driveway. She glides out of the car, and stands so tall she's taller than me. But her slippery sweaty hands squeeze mine like she wants to break my fingers.

"Miss Pasquale! Come along now, or you'll be late!" An older woman all dressed in dark blue stands holding the door to the building open.

"Brave like a bee, Ez," I whisper and she lets my hand go and turns and walks like a queen across the driveway and up the two steps to the front door.

"I ain't never seen that before," Jonagold says and shakes his head. "Every morning the same. Me hauling her, kicking 'n' screaming to that door."

"What's she afraid of?" I ask.

"Muggers, robbers, kidnappers, birds, dogs, lightning, thunder, the sky, rain, basically everything outside the walls of her house," he says and waves me back into the car.

Jonagold drives me back to the Pasquales' house, with me glued to the window for a glance of that amazing fruit shop. The car flies past way too fast this time, but the colors of the fruit make me suck in a deep breath and form a plan to remember how to get back to that shop. I watch all the turns the car makes.

BROKEN HEARTS

That night, when I go up to get Esmeralda's clothes from her bathroom floor, she drags me into the bedroom and sits me on her chair in front of her TV. I think she's going to put on one of those bloopy games again so I stand up. But she pushes me back down.

"What about the plan to get me home?" I ask her.

"I'm going to show you my grandmother. The original Esmeralda Pasquale. The world's finest bee," she says.

Music's coming from the TV. The screen is black and then lights appear. Great circles of light swing across the screen and make themselves into shapes like flowers on the floor. Into the light steps a tiny woman with long,

long legs standing on her very tiptoes. Her hair is shiny black and piled up high on her head, and she wears a yellow-and-black striped singlet, and on her back are long shiny wings. She glides across the floor on her toes, and I suddenly see Ez, today when she stepped from the car. Then the woman lifts her arms and the wings on her back fly up in the air and she swoops and swirls from light flower to light flower.

"Oh," I whisper. "She IS a bee."

"I told you!" Esmeralda says and bounces up and down on the chair beside me. "This dance is called 'The Last Honey Bee,' and this is the best bit!"

The woman leaps into the air and seems to hover, her long straight legs, full of muscles, point in opposite directions, and her arms swoop and glide around her body. Then she lands and bounces back up onto her toes. She dips and she soars like the mud swallows high in the packing shed when Foreman gets his broom out.

"How does she do that?" I ask.

"I know, right?" Esmeralda says, she leaps up and twirls across the front of the TV on her toes. Her hair flies out behind her like glossy black wings.

"You look just like her," I say as Esmeralda spins on the spot. Her face stares at me as her body goes around

120

and then she whips her head around to stare at me again.

"Really?" Esmeralda asks and grins a huge grin as her head whips around again, but then she stops and drops the grin and swoops in to grab my hands from my knees and looks real serious right in my face, me leaning back, coz she's scary like this. "She was kidnapped," Esmeralda whispers. "Bad men took her for ransom, and my dad and his dad paid the money to get her back, but they just killed her anyway."

"Oh," I say.

"My grandfather died of a broken heart," Esmeralda says.

"Oh," I say again, and water fills my eyes coz of my gramps, and how his heart must be aching without me.

"It was a terrible and tragic end to Esmeralda Pasquale," Esmeralda whispers.

I push her upright and stand beside her, grab her shoulders. "But that Esmeralda is not you," I say. "You's brave and you's strong and you's gonna do stuff that's important. Maybe a teacher, maybe a fruit-shop owner, maybe even dance like a bee on a big stage."

Esmeralda pulls her hands away, shaking her head, like I'm lying. "I can't. I can't leave the house!"

"You left the house today. You went to school. You

121

danced into that school looking like a super-cherry dance lady."

"No!" she says. "That was too scary. I can't do more than that." There's tears running down her face.

"You can. And I'll help you," I say.

Esmeralda sniffs. "You will?"

I nod. And now I'm stuck here for as long as it takes, coz Gramps always says, if you promise something, you gotta see it through. Never mind that I promised I'd never leave him. "And you'll help me with a plan to get home," I say.

"I will!" she says. "I just need to figure out Dad's trucks."

KNIVES AND FORKS
IN A ROW

I dump the washing in the washing machine and look around for Ma.

Ivy shoves a smelly plastic bag of rubbish at me and says, "Take this out to the bins at the back."

I screw up my face and take the bag and hold it away on a straight arm as I let myself out the back door and skip across the grass to dump it in the bin as fast as I can.

"No, not tonight." Ma's voice leaks over the wall from the laneway. "I'm tired."

"We'll just go for a little while," the Ape says.

I kick my shoes off and climb a tree beside the wall, then leap for the top of the wall. I land on my chest and elbows and cling on, digging my toes into the cracks between the bricks to keep me there.

The Ape has Ma's arm and is nudging her up the street. She's hanging back, trying to lean on the wall.

"People are expecting us," he says.

"You go on without me," Ma says. "I'm going to check on Peony and go straight to bed."

"It's her, isn't it?" the Ape barks, and twists Ma's arm so she struggles to pull it away. "I knew as soon as she got here, it'd be all about her and you'd have no time for me!"

"It's not like that. I told you, I'm tired!" Ma says.

"Let her go, Slug Face!" I yell down from the wall.

The Ape lets her go and spins around.

"Peony!" Ma says.

"She can't go dizzing me like that all the time!" the Ape yells at Ma. "You need to teach her some respect!" He takes a couple of steps towards the wall like he can jump up and slap me. But I'll be long gone before then.

"Respect this!" I say and hoik a big spit at him. It falls short coz I never been good at spitting.

He looks at the gob on the footpath and his fists ball up. "You!" he says real low.

"Danny, honey sweet," Ma says. "She's just a little girl, she don't mean it." Ma reaches out to take the Ape's arm but he pulls it away from her so hard it sets her stumbling into the wall.

"You can't treat her like that. I'll tell my gramps and he'll knock you into next winter!"

"Peony!" Ma says and stomps back towards the gate.

The Ape eyeballs me and side-eyes Ma, and when she gets to the gate and is distracted by the number machine, he jumps up and slaps at my head. I drop into the garden just as his fingers graze my forehead. "Ha!" I yell as I slide into the skin-scratching bushes.

Ma runs over and hauls me out and squeezes my arm so hard it hurts. She shakes me. "What do you think you're doing?" she yells.

"Stupid females!" the Ape yells over the wall and his footsteps stomp away.

"Now look what you done!" Ma says.

"I'm glad he's gone!" I say. "We're better off without him."

Ma shakes me again and digs her fingers into my arm. "How're we s'posed to make a family if you keep making him mad?" she says.

I rip my arm away. "I don't want to be in a family with him. I want to be in a family with Gramps who has hugs and kind words, and I wanna be in a family with Mags who

125

is strong and always knows how to make me feel good."

"Well, they ain't here!" Ma says and latches on to me again and drags me back towards the house.

"Why would they want to be?" I say.

She pushes me into our washing-machine room and tells me to get in the sink for a wash. She dumps my clothes into the washing machine as I peel them off, and turns it on, then gives me one of her T-shirts to wear to bed. After I'm washed and dried, she drags it over my head, not caring if it pulls my wet hair.

"How come you're nice to Esmeralda but not me?" I ask.

"Caring for Esmeralda is a job," Ma says and shrugs.

"Then what am I?" I ask.

She stops and looks at me. "You know I love you, Peony, but you push my buttons."

I shrug. "I don't know about your buttons," I say.

"It's just something we say. It means you do the opposite of what I want," Ma says.

"Me!" I say and lift my eyebrows way up. "You dragged me away here!"

"Well, now you'll earn money and we'll be able to rent our own little house and stop living like dogs in the dirt," she says.

This makes me burn. "Our shed does us fine!" I shout. "You wanna live in a house like this? All these empty rooms. All this useless stuff! Putting knives and forks the right way on a table?"

"Shh!" Ma says. "This pays your wage."

I flop on the bed and pull the cover over my head. There's no point arguing. I'll be home soon and Ma can carry on her plan without me.

Ma sits down and she strokes the back of my head still sticking out of the cover. "Bloss, please understand. I just want more for all of us. This is a tough old world to be poor in."

"We're not poor, Ma. We're not raggy people in the street. We've got enough." I push the blanket off my face and look at her. "But we've got more if we're all together, taking care of each other."

Ma sighs like she thinks I don't understand. But it's her that don't understand. "When you're older, you'll see," she says. "And you'll be glad you know how to clean a house and earn some cash."

"When I'm older I will be foreman on the farm," I whisper, but I may as well be whispering it to the wall, coz Ma has gone to move the clothes from the machine that washes to the machine that dries.

THE AMAZING EZ

I snuggle into Ma's back while she's sleeping. When I'm gone home, she'll be so angry she'll never lie next to me again. It will be over for us.

When I wake up the next morning, her arm is around me. I kiss her cheek and crawl out. My clothes are folded in a pile, clean and fresh. As I'm pulling them on, Ivy barges through from her room.

"Come on then! Breakfast won't cook itself!" she says.

Ma stirs then, one hand reaches over the edge of the tiny bed, grabbing at the air. I run and pick up the bucket just as she lunges her head over the edge of the bed and vomits.

I hold the bucket and scrape her hair back off her face.

Ma wipes her mouth on the back of her hand and takes a deep breath and looks up at me. "Thank you, Blossom," she says.

I wet a rag and lay it on her forehead before I go into the kitchen to help Ivy.

I can see that Ma needs me. I just can't see that she needs to be here, especially when she's sick every morning. If I go home, she might come too.

Esmeralda asks for me to go to school with her again and everyone's happy to let me go. This helps my promise to Ez and my promise to Gramps, coz nobody minding me coming and going means I'll be able to sneak off real easy.

Ez clings to my arm as we leave the front door and cross to the car. She's holding on tight but jiggling, like she's excited at the same time.

"Ez is a dancing girl who walks like a queen," I whisper and her back straightens and her head lifts and she holds on to my arm with just one hand. Her toes point as she walks. When she gets to the car she forgets she's a queen and throws herself into the back seat in a rush.

I jump in after her.

"What else does Ez do?" she asks.

I think for a while. "Ez is a girl who likes to run through fields of golden grass, under wide blue skies, with her black hair flowing out behind. Sometimes Ez runs so fast she catches up to a mob of roos and they all run together, wheeling and swooping, leaping fences and startling cows, making them bellow, 'MooOOOoo!' and then she laughs like a kookaburra, 'Kaa, kaa, kaa, koo kooo!'"

Ez laughs too, and changes it to be more like a kookaburra, then she says, "But does Ez get hot from all that running?"

I nod. "She gets so hot she runs to a dam. She leaps straight for the middle and bombs water everywhere and swims in circles, never mind that ducks quack at her and the yabbies nip at her toes. 'Stop tickling me!' she tells them, then she runs again through the wide golden fields to dry out. And when she runs past the farms, all the children and the farm dogs see her running and want to run too."

"I'm afraid of dogs."

"Ez isn't. She loves dogs and they love her. They see the happiness in her face and know that she is part wild thing like them. Something wild that likes to run just to feel free. So all the farm dogs and all the farm children come out to run with wild Ez for a while, but none of them can keep up with her."

"Does Ez dance?"

"Ez dances. She dances under the full moon on the highest hill, and everyone sees her and climbs the hill to watch, and musicians come with their guitars and drums and try to make music that's as good as Ez's dances, and people see Ez dance, and hear the music, and they're so happy, they all dance too, spinning round and around. Ez dances so beautiful that everyone forgets their troubles, forgets that they're hungry, forgets that they're old and their backs don't bend so good no more. They throw away their walking sticks and dance like toddlers, leaping about, laughing, holding hands. Everyone under the moonlight, with Ez at the middle, on the very top of the hill, with the moon big and glowing behind her."

"Wow!" Ez says.

I smile.

"But what happens when Ez stops dancing?" Ez asks.

"Then everyone stops dancing, and they look at each other like maybe they were under a magic spell. 'Please, Miss Ez,' they call, 'dance for us some more?' And Ez says, 'Next full moon. But right now I have to go to school and learn to read real good.'"

Ez looks out the car window at the dark brick building. "How did we get here so fast?"

I cup my hand around her ear and whisper, "Ez magic."

"Here?" Jonagold asks when we're still four cars from the closest park to the door.

"Closer!" Esmeralda says.

"Ez, who's brave and wild and likes to run, wouldn't say 'closer,'" I whisper.

Esmeralda frowns.

"I'll run with you. We'll run to the door like wild things. Nuthin' can touch us, coz nuthin' can keep up with us," I say.

"Here, Jonagold, here!" Ez says.

I jump out the door, hold out my hand. "Come on, Ez!"

She slides over, takes my hand and we run. Up the path I tow her, around the corner, and up to the school door. Her hair streams out behind her. My stupid shoes slap and slam and slow me down, and I wish my feet were wild and bare.

The woman waiting in the blue suit steps back as we thump into the door. Ez is laughing and gasping for air. "Miss Esmeralda!" the woman says. "That is not how young women arrive at this school!"

"You's not a young woman," I whisper. "You's wild and running like the wind."

The woman scowls down at me, but Jonagold is calling me back. He's holding out Ez's schoolbag we left lying on the seat.

I run back and get it and carry it over my shoulder to Ez. "Make sure you dance today," I say and give it to her. She smiles and ducks through the door.

The woman in the blue suit has her finger out like she's gonna tell me off for something, but she's not my boz. I got more than enough of those with Ivy and the Pasquales, so I run back to Jonagold and the car.

UNDER THE WIDE BLUE SKY

I wait, holding open the Pasquales' front door after school, and Jonagold waits, holding open the car door.

Ez sits, peering out, like there's a river of crocodiles to cross.

"Come on, Miss Esmeralda," Jonagold says, holding out his hand.

Ez just stares.

"Hmmpf," Jonagold grumbles like he's given up waiting, and reaches in to grab Ez.

"Don't!" I say. "Don't you touch Miss Ez! She don't need a lump like you wrapping their big ugly paws round her arm!"

"Hey!" Jonagold says, but he stands up.

I kick off my shoes and use them to prop the door open, and run over to the car. "Miss Ez is just waiting for the music to be just right." I hum the music I heard when her grandmother did the bee dance. The music for "The Last Honey Bee."

Jonagold's frowning at me, but then he sees Ez sliding closer to the door, pointing one toe out. He steps back, and taps along to the tune with his fingertips on the door of the car. I point my toes in my stupid white socks and hold my arms up like I saw on the TV and take little dancing steps across the courtyard to the front door, humming all the time.

Ez gets out of the car, bobs real low with her arms out and then walks, first long-legged steps with her toes pointed out, then jiggly little steps on her toes.

She smiles and twirls past me into the front hallway. Jonagold has to carry her bag in and give it to me, coz queens don't carry their own bags, do they?

"Thanks," he says, like I'm doing him a favor.

I grab my shoes and hurry after Ez who's already starting up the stairs. I put her bag down. "Ez?" I say. "Come to the kitchen, I got a surprise for you."

"What?" she asks.

"You'll see." I run on my slippery socks across the wooden floor through the door to the white-tiled kitchen.

Esmeralda follows me. "Did Ivy make my favorite?" she asks.

I nod. "Passionfruit sponge," I say. Never mind I've never even heard of that till Ivy told me.

Ez looks at the bare bench and at Ivy standing there with her hands on her hips. "Where?" she asks.

I grab her hand and pull her to the kitchen window. Down on the lawn sits a blanket with the cake waiting beside pretty plates.

Esmeralda shakes her head. "I can't do picnics," she says.

"Ez would," I say. "Ez would pull off her shoes and run down that green grass and eat a huge slice of cake."

"Can we picnic inside?" Esmeralda asks.

"It is inside. It's inside your beautiful garden surrounded by a high wall and a locked gate and it's perfectly safe." I pull off my socks and scrunch them into my shoes. "Come on, wild Ez," I say.

She kicks off her shoes, takes off her socks one by one and rolls them slowly and puts them inside her shoes. I throw open the kitchen door.

"Flies!" Ivy grumbles as I take Ez's hand and lead her

down the steps and along the house wall. She keeps one hand on the house like she needs to be close to it, and at the corner where she has to let go and start down the lawn, she freezes and shakes her head.

"Brave, strong Ez runs like this!" I say and I take off running a big circle on the lawn, my arms out like a plane, and it's nice to have bare feet. It's good to feel the soft grass on the soles of my feet, and how my feet bend and push. I laugh and run a lap right past Ez. "Follow me!" I call and she lets go of the wall then grabs it again, like she's dizzy. I run another lap. "Run with me!" I call. Ez lets go of the house and runs out onto the lawn, picking up her feet like the cool grass is strange, like she has to tiptoe-run on it.

"Ooh, it's soft," she says.

"Run like the wind!" I yell, running past her again.

She holds her arms out and runs after me. We lap big circles of the garden.

"I've never been down here!" Ez yells.

"Run!" I yell, and we lap the garden again.

We fall onto the blanket gasping for breath. I lie on my back. "Ez!" I whisper. "Lie down, look up at the wide blue sky!"

She does. "I feel sick," she says. "It's too empty!"

"It's not empty, it's full of blue and clouds," I say. "Look there, that one is a dog."

Esmeralda sits up. "I don't like dogs. I don't like open spaces. Take me back to the house."

I wave my hands up at the sky. "Ez runs through golden fields under the wide blue sky. She's not afraid of anything."

"But I'm afraid! Take me up to the house!" Esmeralda says.

PASSIONFRUIT CAKE

I sit up and look at her. "You don't have to look at the sky. Look at the cake Ivy made."

"Take me back up to the house. I'm too scared to go alone," Esmeralda says.

I cross my legs like I've got all day. "You were really brave when you let the house go and just ran."

"Peony! You have to do what I say!" Esmeralda says.

"Nah," I say. "I think I'm going to sit here and eat this big ol' picnic cake. If you don't want any, I'll eat the whole thing. I never had a cake like this before." I pull the cake over to me, and use the slicer to heft a big slice of it onto my plate.

Esmeralda is fuming hot beside me. Her lips are sucked in tight, like she's trying to stop from yelling at me.

I pull the slice apart in the middle and shove it into my mouth. It's sweet and fruity-fragrant and there's silky cream in the middle, and super sweet icing on top. "Thith ith amathing!" I say around the cake in my mouth.

"You eat like a pig!" Ez says. She sticks out her finger, scoops a hunk of cream out of the middle of the cake and wipes it on my nose.

"Hey!" I say, looking from the big dent in the cream on the perfect cake to the blob of white on my nose. "You can't do that!"

"I don't have to do what you say!" Ez says and digs her fingers into the edge of the cake, picks up a lump and holds it like she's about to slam it into my face.

I jump up. "No! Ez, this is the best cake ever! Don't waste it!"

Ez jumps up too and runs around the edge of the blanket with the cake in her hand. "Are you afraid of it?" she asks, and she bites a hunk out of the middle of the cake. Cream rings her mouth. She licks her lips. "Want some?" she says and shoves it at me.

"No!" I yell and run. She chases me, around and around the lawn, laughing like a kookaburra.

"You's crazy!" I yell and run back to the house, coz that's the only thing that's going to make her stop.

She trips me before I get to the paving. I hit the grass and roll onto my back, and she crawls on top of me, shoving the cake at my face, and I can't waste it, even if it's too sweet, so I bite it and eat it as fast as a hungry dog, but she's shoving it so hard it spreads out over my cheeks.

"Eg, margh!" I yell but I have to chew and swallow, and squirm my head back and forth to even breathe.

A clip-clopping sound stops my heart dead. Ez sits up. I look up at Mrs. Pasquale, in her tall shoes, her pulled-back hair, her stitched-on dress, her frown.

"What!" she yells, then takes a deep breath and makes her voice tight and quiet. "What are you doing?"

"Thorry, Ma'am," I say and scramble out from under Ez.

THE PICNIC

"Peony and me are having a picnic," Ez says and points a cake-messy hand down the lawn to the blanket which is still laid out nice like I set it.

Mrs. Pasquale looks down the lawn to the blanket, then back to Ez who's acting like she goes outside every day.

Mrs. Pasquale turns around to Ivy who's standing at the back door. Ivy jumps and ducks back into the kitchen. Mrs. Pasquale sighs.

Now I'm sure she's gonna slap me, and pull me by my ear, and chuck me out that gate onto the street with the raggy people.

But she just says, "Peony and *I* are having a picnic,"

which is confusing, coz the last thing I want to do is have a picnic with Mrs. Pasquale, who's probably mad as a snake caught up in Foreman's mower about the mess, but hiding it good.

She yells, "Ivy, bring towels and a kitchen chair!

"May I join your picnic?" she asks Esmeralda, even though it's really my picnic.

Esmeralda smiles. "Yes, you may," she says.

Ivy brings a chair down to the blanket and hands us both some towels. We wipe our faces and hands.

We sit cross-legged on the blanket opposite Mrs. Pasquale perched on the kitchen chair.

"Look at the color of your feet!" Mrs. Pasquale says.

"We's wild!" Esmeralda says.

Mrs. Pasquale nods. "We *are* wild," she says, never mind there's nothing wild about Mrs. Pasquale in her perfect clothes.

"Can you cut me a slice of cake, Peony?" Mrs. Pasquale says.

I cut a slice for her from the side Ez didn't touch and then slice Ez a real piece from the bit she did touch. I finish my piece as Mrs. Pasquale asks Ez questions about school and never once asks her how she got to be outside without panicking.

"Did you go to school back home, Peony?" Mrs. Pasquale asks me.

"Only radio school," I say. "Coz we're too busy with the fruit. They'll be missing me something bad. I'm a pest, with my sister Mags, we're a real good team with our chooks, but I'm gonna be a bee real soon. Almost made it last time. And I help my friend Applejoy look after his little brother. His ma isn't very strong. He's already a bee, got a shiny yellow-and-black vest an' everything." I wanna make Mrs. Pasquale see how important it is for me to get back, but she holds up a hand.

"My goodness you talk quickly," she says, like she hasn't heard anything I said. Or maybe what I say isn't important enough to listen to. "It's so nice out here in the garden. Was it your idea to have a picnic?"

I nod.

Mrs. Pasquale smiles. "It's a good idea. We should do it more often." She stands up and hands me her empty plate. "I have work to do, but please stay out here as long as you'd like." She kisses Ez on the top of the head before she totters back up the lawn on her tall heels.

"I thought she was gonna hit me, when she saw me with cake all over," I whisper to Ez.

"Ha!" Ez says. "Mum doesn't hit anyone."

144

"What about your pa?"

"Dad? Never. He just bosses us all around," Ez says and I wonder how it is that she's never seen her dad hit Ma. Ez stands up. "Please come with me back to the house. I'm worried it's going to get dark soon."

I wave at the house where Ivy and Ma are watching from the window. "It's right there. Brave Ez can run there quick as anything. Strong Ez can carry the blanket while I carry the plates and Ivy's cake," I say, not trusting her with what's left of this precious sweet thing.

I stand up and pick up the plates and slicer while Ez collects the blanket, rolls it up all messy, and we walk up to the house.

"Flies!" Ivy calls when we step into the kitchen. Then, "Your feet!" Ez laughs so hard, she stumbles into me and I have to put the cake on the bench before I drop it.

I still have to go up and collect Ez's washing even though I worked hard enough getting that picnic together.

"That was so much fun!" Ez says, standing in a towel next to a whole bathtub full of warm water. A bath so big it could fit me, Mags, AJ and little Mango all at once. Seems like a waste of all that warm water for just one girl. I've half a mind to leap in there and swim about like a fish. "Let's do that every afternoon," she says.

"It's not warm every afternoon," I say. "And anyway, I can't, coz my Gramp's heart is breaking from me being here instead of with him. I have to get home."

Esmeralda nods and pushes her smile straight. "I said I'd help you," she says. "What I think is, you have to get on one of the fruit trucks going from the coolstore to Goulburn Valley. I've checked out the maps and there's a corner near my school where the trucks will turn off if they're going to Goulburn Valley. You just have to get on one when it stops at the traffic lights."

"How will I do that?" I ask.

"I'll cause a scene. I'm very good at causing a scene. When everyone is looking at me, you'll slip onto the truck." Esmeralda shrugs and tilts her head to the side like she knows just how smart she is.

And she is smart! "You's super-cherries, Ez!" I say, and she laughs.

She scrapes together her wad of clothes off the floor and shoves them at me. "Here's my washing. You better get that downstairs before anyone finds out you're up here planning things."

HALFWAY

The next day on the way to school, Ez sucks in a deep breath at the front door, and strides out pointing her toes all the way to the car soon as Jonagold opens the door.

"Good morning, Miss Esmeralda," he says as she jumps into the back seat. I follow along with Ez's bag.

Near her school, she points down a street and whispers, "It's just down there, where the trucks go past. I'll get you there, tomorrow."

Once through the school gates, Ez just says, "Park anywhere, Jonagold."

"So brave," I say. Jonagold parks a long way from the front door.

"You have to walk with me," Ez whispers as I open the door.

"Halfway," I say. "And you can carry your bag."

Ez frowns at me.

But I frown right back. "Stop thinking about it, and do it."

When I get out of the car, she pulls her bag over her shoulder and pushes past me, so I'm not even walking with her, just walking along behind. I stop halfway.

She takes a few steps and turns and looks back at me.

"Be strong, Ez," I say, me thinking tomorrow I'll be off so she'll have to manage alone.

She nods, hefts her bag and strides on again. "Hi, Esmeralda!" a girl with long blonde hair calls and runs to catch up with her. I watch her walk into school just like all the other girls. At the door, she turns and waves.

Later, Ma's setting the table for the Pasquales' dinner. She picks up each knife and fork and polishes it with a cloth before she lays it on the table. They get two knives and two forks each and a spoon. Ma's not even bothering to notice the different sizes of the knives and the forks, and she's not putting the smallest on the outside.

"Ma," I say, and I move a little knife to the outside.

"Thought you said this wasn't important," Ma says.

"Thought you said the Pasquales like things how they like them," I say. "I don't want Mr. Pasquale to hit you coz you can't remember how the knives go."

"Nah," she says. "I'm just clumsy-tired all the time. Bang into things. Don't you worry 'bout it."

"But Ma," I say. "You can come home to rest."

"Stop going on, Peony," Ma snaps. "My job is here. My man is here. You are here. This is my life. Here."

I shake my head. "But how can you have a life when Gramps and Mags are somewhere else?"

Ma hurries back to the kitchen with me trailing behind. "They're fine there. That's where they want to be."

"That's where I want to be too," I say.

Ivy shoves a bowl into my hands. Tiny red perfect tomatoes and little black olives and tiny white square cheeses, sitting on a pile of green. "Quit nagging your ma and put the salad on the table," she says and turns me around, pushes me back to the dining room.

Mr. Pasquale is coming down the stairs so I shut up and hurry to the table.

"Peony," he calls.

I stop.

"I hear you've been helping our Esmeralda?" he says.

"Yes, sir," I say.

"Jonagold says Esmeralda walked to the car by herself, and my wife says she was playing in the garden with you," he says.

I nod. I'm still not sure if I'm in trouble coz of the cake mess.

"Thank you," he says, and he digs in his pocket. He holds out a blue note. Ten whole dollars!

My hand is out and taking it before I even know it.

"Something extra," he whispers. "Just for you, for working extra hard."

I hold the ten dollars back out to him. "I'm not doing it as part of work," I say. "I'm doing it coz I promised Ez I would."

Mr. Pasquale waves his hand. "Then you definitely deserve it. Keeping promises can be hard sometimes."

I nod. This is something I know for sure.

HER GRANDMOTHER'S WALK

The next day, when the car gets out the gate and onto the road on the way to school, even though Esmeralda's hands are sweaty, gripping mine, she says confident as anything to Jonagold, "Take Forrester Road on the way to school today. I want to show Peony our trucks, and they always refuel at that servo on the way out of town." She turns and winks at me.

Jonagold is probably just happy without all Esmeralda's fussing, coz he agrees right away.

I squeeze Ez's hand. My own hands are gonna be sweating soon.

Jonagold pulls the car up alongside the servo and

drums his fingers on the steering wheel. Cars are filing in and out, but out the back there is a line of trucks waiting to refuel, or parked. Some have the green pear and two orange apricots of my farm on them.

"Those are ours," Esmeralda says, "and that one with the red cab, and that one." Then she drops her voice to a whisper and points to the traffic lights ahead. "If they turn right there, they're going to Goulburn Valley."

I nod. "Thanks, Ez," I say.

"Go," she whispers. She pushes a plastic bag into my hand, pulls the lock button on her door open, and reaches for the handle. The plan is going down now. Right now!

We both leap into the street and I run straight towards the servo, to get lost in the cars and trucks.

Jonagold yells behind me. I glance over my shoulder. Ez is running in the opposite direction, but there's a group of shops up that way and raggy people waiting at the doors, begging with their hands out. Is she going to run right past them and into a shop?

I keep running for the trucks, slip around behind the nearest one, duck down by a tyre and look around to see where the drivers are. Most of them are chatting in a group near the pumps.

The plastic bag clunks on the concrete. I open it up.

152

A can of bubbly drink sits in there, and a round pink and yellow apple. A whole apple, all for me.

I don't know whether to hug it, eat it all in a rush, or keep it to show AJ and Mags when I get home. I'm thinking I should definitely keep it to share with AJ and Mags. But there's a little cry from up the street. Ez!

Ez has almost reached the shops but she hasn't had the courage to push through the raggy people. She's stopped, frozen. Even from here, the trembling shake of her body tells me she can't go on.

Jonagold is busy locking the car, waving one hand at the people beeping their car behind him, like they're telling him to get the car off the road.

The raggy people turn, and shuffle towards Esmeralda.

I look up at the truck, at my beautiful green pear and apricots sign.

I could get on and be on my way home.

I run towards Ez.

The raggy people are in a circle around Ez by the time I get to her. Her arms are pulled in tight against her chest, her eyes squeezed tight shut, and her skin has turned grey and stiff. I think she might be dead. Standing up dead.

I push through the people, push away their limp reaching hands. "Ez!" I say.

She whimpers and trembles.

Hands nudge at her. "Miss, please." "Miss, can you spare something." "Just a little food." "Just a few coins." I pull my ten dollars out of my pocket and lift it high. Hands snatch at it, and the empty air. I take out my can of bubbly drink, and lift it up to the snatching hands. Finally, I take out my beautiful pink and yellow apple, and long fingers with dirty nails wrap around it, and it's gone.

"That's all!" I shout. "That's all we have!" and the people step back, a little, give us some room. I take Esmeralda's hands in mine.

"Ez, these people are just hungry. They don't want to hurt you."

Ez's eyes flap open, so round the whites make great circles around the dark brown of her irises.

"Ez!" I whisper in Ez's ear. "You's brave like a bee, take my hand and we'll walk back to the car. You are Esmeralda Pasquale, the one who is alive and strong."

Esmeralda grips my hand harder, her neck grows long, her chin tucks in, she points a toe and takes a step, and then another. I let her lead me. Then she drops my hand and walks alone.

Jonagold arrives, and pushes through the people. "Get back, give her some room!"

She walks through the gap he's made.

Jonagold hurries alongside and then runs ahead to open the car door.

Esmeralda glides in like a duck on a dam.

"Where were you going?" Jonagold says, his face red and angry.

"Just to get a closer look at the trucks," I say.

"Where was *she* going?" he asks.

"I dunno," I say.

"Humpf!" he grunts, and jumps back in the car before the raggy people come to pound on the windows.

Esmeralda's shaking all over as the car moves back into the traffic.

"You – you came back for me!" she whispers. "You were away, but you came back."

I nod. "You needed help."

She smiles. "You're a good friend."

"You're a good friend," I say, "coz even though you's scared you still tried to help me."

Esmeralda lets out a sigh. "We will be friends forever. And if I ever get a fruit farm, I'm going to put you in charge of it."

I laugh and nod, and I think this is a thing that could happen.

At the school, I get out with Esmeralda and she squeezes my hand and does her grandmother's walk all the way to the front door.

Jonagold is shaking his head in the front when I get back in the car. "I don't know what you two are up to."

That afternoon when we collect Esmeralda from school she whispers to me, "I've had an idea. Can you walk from the school to the servo?"

"Easy," I say.

"Then we'll lose Jonagold in the school. That way I won't get in your way again," she says.

I poke her on the nose. "You," I say, "is never in my way. You's the one person here on my side."

She laughs. "I'm going to miss you. But once you're safely home, I'm going to make Rosie tell me where you live and then come and visit you."

"You'd come all that way?" I ask.

"I'm getting braver all the time!" she says and shoves me like Mags might.

I laugh and shove her back.

LOOK AT THE MAGIC

The next day, soon as we get in the car, Ez whispers, "Not today, because Jonagold's watching us after yesterday. We'll try on Monday." I nod.

She don't even need me to walk halfway with her to the school. She steps out of the car, looks up and down the school path, sticks her chin up and walks like nothing can stop her getting to that school door.

Jonagold stands smiling at the front of the car, him not even needing to open the door for her, and tips his hat as she passes, like he just saw a real queen.

"I reckon you're an angel, young Peony," he says when we get in the car to drive back to the house.

"Cha!" I say, coz angels are silly things in white dresses. "I'm a bee."

That night, Ez is up late coz she says there's no school tomorrow. She's watching her TV in her room when I go up to collect her washing. It's a program about wolves and shows one howling at the moon.

"Look, Peony!" she says. "That's the moon like in the story about Ez dancing."

Here's a girl dressed in fluffy flowers sitting in a huge room all alone looking at a picture of a big glorious moon.

I laugh. I double over, holding my belly, cawing like a galah.

"What?" Ez says.

I grab her arm and tow her to the window, pull back the heavy curtains and point.

The moon is low and huge. Shining right down on Ez's own back yard.

"Come on, wild Ez, now it's your turn!" I grab her hand and pull her tripping and toe-stubbing down the stairs, through the kitchen and out the back door. She's grabbing things, saying, "Wait!" and Ivy's calling, "What's going on?" and, "Flies!"

"Waaait!" Ez howls again, but I'm not slowing down enough for her to get a grip on nuthin'.

"I'm gonna see you dance in the moonlight, Miss Ez!" I yell.

In the middle of the lawn I let her go.

"Peony!" she yells, so angry. "I can't be out here!"

Faces arrive at the windows of the house, she's yelling so loud.

"Ez dances under the light of the full moon, and people come to see her dance, come to see the magic that makes them happy," I say. "Please, Miss Ez, dance for us, they say. Dance so we can forget our worries."

"It's too dark! Take me back to the house!" Ez says, reaching for my arm, her being too scared to be completely angry at me.

"Musicians come to play, old people throw away their walking sticks, when they see the joy in Ez's face," I say, and I hum the tune I remember from the dance of "The Last Honey Bee."

"Peony, please," Ez whispers.

"Dance, Ez, dance!" I say, and go back to humming.

Ez takes a deep breath, lifts her arms and steps away from me. Then she stops, drops her arms and looks around.

"Ez, you's a bee. You's the bravest thing in the world. You's the last honey bee," I whisper.

She takes a step again and twirls, dips and lifts.

"Ez dances under the light of the full moon," I call, and she lifts her arms like she can catch the moon right out of the dark sky.

A window opens, up at the house, and the real music of "The Last Honey Bee" floats down the lawn, wraps itself under Ez's arms, lifts her up.

"And the musicians come to play for her!" I call. "And all the people come to watch!"

Ez spins and looks up to the house, where Mr. and Mrs. Pasquale stand at the upstairs open window, and Ivy and Ma stand at the kitchen window.

"Show them the joy on your face as you dance from flower to flower, Ez!" I call. She leaps and dips and runs on pointed toes. I kick off my stupid shoes and chase after her, imitating her moves. But I really am the bee, running along tree limbs on my tippy-toes, reaching to touch each imaginary flower.

"And the people forget their worries and dance along!" I call.

When I look up a moment later, Mr. and Mrs. Pasquale are coming out the back door, holding hands.

Then they face each other. Mr. Pasquale holds out his arms and Mrs. Pasquale steps into them. He puts a hand around her back, and holds her hand in his, so softly, then he steps and spins her around, and they've got their own kind of dance, a dance for two. I never seen two people dance like that before. So gentle, so together.

Ivy and Ma step out of the kitchen and they hold each other too. Clumsy-stepping and loose-holding like they're kids copying the Pasquales. They're all laughing, all dancing in the yellow light from the kitchen, in the pale light of the large low moon. They've really all forgotten their worries.

I run and grab Ez. "Look!" I whisper. "Look at your magic!"

Ez laughs. She runs and twirls and spins around the dancing grown-ups. Everybody laughing. Everybody moving differently but still in time to the music. Not a worry to be seen.

But I'm not dancing, no more, coz I still got worries. All this talk of bees just brings my problems crowding round me like hungry raggy people.

I gotta get back to the farm.

SORRY SAD

After I dump Esmeralda's clothes in the washing machine, I look for Ma but can't find her. Ivy is there, fussing.

"Girl, come help me with deliveries!" She bustles me out to the side gate and punches the numbers.

A man in a red shirt is standing next to a red van.

"Hold the gate open," Ivy tells me and she goes to where the man is stacking up boxes on a little handcart.

"Want me to bring them in for you?" he asks.

"The Pasquales don't allow anyone in that they don't personally invite," Ivy says and grabs the handle of the hand cart. She hauls it past, with me flat against the gate holding it open for her, and the man looks at me and shrugs.

I shrug back.

Up the street, a woman cries out and the delivery driver takes a few steps in that direction. "What... that man just hit that woman," he says.

I let the gate go and run. I run hard as I can. Legs flying like on the farm. My stupid hard shoes don't make it easy, but I'm fair moving when I hit the Ape side on, with my knees up and driving into his rib cage. He staggers sideways and falls and I'm on top of him, pounding at his face with my fists and they're too small to do anything so I bring a foot up and stomp his face a couple of times, with my stupid shoe, before he grabs me and throws me off.

I scrape the heels of my hands and one elbow when I hit the concrete.

He sits up red and raging.

"Don't you lay a hand on my ma!" I scream. My own red raging is way stronger than his, even if my fists are not.

"P, please!" Ma whimpers, lying on the footpath.

I run to her and help her get up. The Ape looms over both of us.

The delivery driver arrives on thumping boots and shoves him back with, "What do you think you're doing?"

"Ma, come on," I say, dragging at her, in a hurry to get her up.

Ivy arrives puffing and panting. "Come on, Rosie," she says in her bossy voice. "Let's get you inside and cleaned up." She takes Ma's other arm and we get her moving a couple of steps. It was the Ape! It was always the Ape hitting Ma, never Ivy, never the Pasquales.

"Rosie!" the Ape yells, like he's yelling her name from a mountaintop.

Ma stops and looks back, and when me and Ivy tug at her again she pulls her arms from our grips.

"You walk away from me now and it's over!" Ape yells at her, his face red and trembling.

"Danny," Ma whimpers.

"No!" he yells. "You choose now. Me," he stabs his fat gorilla finger at me, "or her."

"You don't need that no-hoper," Ivy whispers in Ma's ear and takes her arm again.

Ma don't move.

"Me or her!" the Ape yells.

"Ma," I whisper and take her hand. She pulls it back. I grab it again. "Come home," I plead, coz even though she makes me mad day after day, she's my ma and there ain't no life for her with him.

164

She pulls her hand away again, and whimpers, "Danny!"

"Rosie, no," Ivy pleads.

Ma walks away from us. She walks towards the Ape. And when she gets there, she doesn't punch him in the face like I hope she will. She wraps her arms around him like he is the only one who can save her. And it sinks on me slowly that she's leaving me behind.

Ivy's worked it out. She wraps both arms around me and pulls me so close my back sinks into her belly.

"No!" I scream at Ma. "We're family, Ma! I'd fight for you, always! Come home!"

The Ape pulls Ma away down the road.

Ma glances back, she's crying. Tears roll down her face. She sniffs. "I'll come back for my stuff, Ivy," she says.

"Ma!" I scream. But she won't look at me.

Ivy hauls me back to the kitchen. She feeds me sweet tea and puts me to bed.

"She'll be back," Ivy says, "she always comes back."

In the morning, Ma is not back. She's still not back by the time I go to school with Esmeralda.

I'm heavy-hearted and sorry sad, like I really did something bad to Ma, but I can't think what. And now I'm leaving and Ma ain't here to stop me. And she probably won't come after me. I'm lost in the world. I sit in the car and squeeze Esmeralda's hand real tight. This time for me.

"Can Peony just walk me to the door?" Esmeralda asks.

We're early and Jonagold has got the car right up close to the school and he's grinning when he says, "Sure thing, Miss Esmeralda."

Ez laughs and pulls me from the car. I walk with her to the school door, holding her hand.

"Are you ready to go home?" she asks, looking past me at Jonagold waiting.

I nod. I'm ready more than ever. Nothing to keep me here no more.

LAUGHING LIKE A KOOKABURRA

Esmeralda smiles her most brilliant smile, laughs and pulls me in through the school doors. She runs down the pale corridors laughing like a kookaburra, towing me along the shiny floors, past classrooms filled with bright artwork. Our shoes clatter up a storm.

"Miss Pasquale!" someone calls after her.

We skid around a corner and down another corridor. Then we reach a revolving door. Esmeralda takes a card from her pocket and swipes the door panel and pushes me into the gap.

"It only goes out. From here, you're on your own."

She pulls a plastic bag from her schoolbag and shoves it at me.

I reach back and hug her, then take the plastic bag.

"Thank you, Ez," I say. "You's cherries all the way. The best Esmeralda Pasquale ever."

I push through the revolving door, down a path, through a revolving one-way gate and back into the street. First thing I do is take off my stupid shoes and socks and sit them up on a wall. I think a homeless person with small feet will be glad to find them sitting there.

I run across the road and the three blocks down to the turn-off to the servo. And there they are, all the trucks, all lined up, chrome and paint gleaming in the morning sun. Bright and real and waiting to take me home.

I check back for the intersection where the truck has to turn right. Try to get that direction in my head. Then I choose the nearest truck with my pear and apricots on the side.

There's no driver in it, no one looking. It has canvas sides so I loosen off one of the catches and crawl up under the canvas. I don't bother tightening it again coz if the truck takes the wrong turn I might need to get out in a hurry. There's a pallet cart in here, tied tight to the floor, but the rest of the back is empty, same as it would be if it was heading to my farm. It's good so far. I sit on the pallet cart and jiggle my knees and wait.

The driver's boots sound on the concrete. He yells, "See ya!" to someone and the cab door creaks open. The truck leans a little and the door slams, sending my heart jumping in my chest. If that driver can't hear my heart through that wall then he must be deaf!

The truck starts up and rolls forwards. I jump up and run back to where I loosened off the canvas.

It's hard running on a moving truck deck, almost as hard as being a bee on a branch in the wind, but at least with bare feet, my toes can spread and feel the moving floor under them.

I lie on my belly and the truck goes down the dip of the servo driveway and pulls out onto the road. When it slows at the intersection I push the canvas open and watch the road below. We're in the lane on the right-hand side, and when the truck takes off it swings around to the right. I'm going home. I'm going back to the Goulburn Valley. Back to Gramps and Mags and AJ. I smile and plant a kiss on the truck floor, then spit the dirt from my lips.

JIGGLING AND
WORRYING

I'm pretty sure days have passed with me pacing up and down, and sitting on the forks of the pallet cart, jiggling and worrying, but the sun is still high in the sky, it's not gone down once since I got on. I open the plastic bag Ez gave me and in there is a little bottle of apple juice and a packet of potato chips. I guzzle the apple juice, coz it's hot here under the canvas, and then I eat the chips. The salt makes my throat thirsty all over again. "Silly Ez," I mutter, even though I'm pleased she thought to give me something. Every time the truck slows, I run to the gap in the canvas and check what's going on out there.

We've been in the countryside for ages, but the last time I checked it was finally the right kind of countryside. I don't need no phone or address to tell me this is the place I belong. We've gone past the rolling yellow fields of canola flowers, past the wide flat plains of yellow stalks on dust, where the air was so dry it made my nostrils ache, and now the air has a bit more moisture, and the land has edges to it. Hills and creeks. The autumn grass, burned off by summer, waits to be mowed to hay. Vines and fruit trees stand in rows. My head is busting with the happiness that I am home. But where is my farm and when can I get off this truck?

There's a whole lot more wiggling and worrying before the truck grinds to a halt. I think it's probably at a farm, or somewhere I can ask the people that work there where is the farm on Something Creek Road that Foreman runs.

It's just another servo, but I can't wait no more. I slip out, and land on the hot concrete alongside the truck.

"Get away, you," the driver yells and shoves me. "There's no fruit on this one for you to steal."

"I wasn't," I say, but the driver is already walking towards the servo building.

I walk out to the edge of the concrete and the land

171

feels right. It feels like home. I could hike out from here but I need to know which way to go.

There's a tap next to the diesel pump so I go and get myself a drink of water. I turn the tap off when the driver comes back from passing the money in through the servo hatch.

"How far to the farm on Something Creek Road, where Foreman runs it?" I ask.

"Foreman who?" he asks.

And I try to think of a name. Just as the driver gives up and turns away, I remember Foreman's last name.

"Mahase!" I say.

The driver squints his eyes and searches the sky for a while. "Yeah... Broken Creek Road, I reckon. The Foreman's big, one eyebrow." The driver draws a line right across his forehead with his finger so I understand it's really two eyebrows joined together.

"Yes!" I say, and I can't help hopping from foot to foot on the hot concrete. "Are you going there?"

"No. I'm going straight on. You need to go about thirty kays in that direction." He points across the paddock behind the servo.

"Thanks!" I say and set off.

"Where you going?" he calls.

"Home!" I say.

"You can't just walk thirty kays in this heat!" he yells.

"Yes, I can!" I yell back.

SWEET HONEY GIRL

The rest of the day, I walk through the dry autumn grass. My feet healed from my last run through the stubbly grass but now they're soft from being trapped in the stupid hard shoes. I climb fences and search out creeks to drink from, and to cool my burning bare feet.

I walk through the hot late afternoon sun and into the evening, until it gets dark and then I find a log to sleep next to. I push my back against it and pull my knees up to my chest. I wake when the bats go over, circling the trees over me, calling to each other. The noise isn't so scary as gun bangs down the street in the dark. I call out like a bat, lonely in the night, but no one will be answering me.

My stomach is sucked in against my backbone when I wake with the sun in my eyes. I walk to a creek and try to fill my emptiness up with water.

"This is juicy pig on bread," I tell my stomach. "You still eating higher than a king, little stomach," I tell it. It gurgles back like it knows I'm lying. Trucks roar in the distance so I leave the creek and head out across a wide dusty paddock. I'm thinking maybe they're fruit trucks heading up to farms and maybe one is going to my farm.

I pass through a field full of vines, and stop to suck at the irrigation pipes dripping water onto the vine roots. It's not enough water, but it's something. I walk on down a hill and back up, following that roar on the road.

The problem with heading the way the fruit trucks are heading is I'm getting further and further from the creek that wound in and out of my path yesterday.

The sun beats down on my back, and burns my arms and face and the top of my head right through my hair. I take off my good black trousers and wrap them around my head for a while, and keep my eyes mostly closed against the glare, and the trucks keep roaring on past down on the highway. In the late afternoon, the trucks are roaring the other way and I'm so hot I think I'm gonna melt. My tongue is fat and dry in my mouth and my legs are so wobbly I keep falling down. I get to a fence and rest against it for ages before I find the strength to squeeze through the wires. There's some shade on the other side hard up against the fence in the long grass that grows all matted there, so I lie down and sleep.

The next morning my lips are glued together and my tongue is stuck to the roof of my mouth. Still, the trucks start up their rumbling down on the road, and it makes me push myself up so my bare feet can plod on. My feet are sore, scraped and cut, and each step stabs up through my legs. Every bit of me is sore, but as long as I keep moving I have a chance. A chance to get home. The sun gets higher and hotter and my legs get wobbly again. My head aches and I think I'm gonna die out here if I don't find a creek soon, but I can't think which way to look for one so I keep walking the way the trucks are going.

A man yells and I can't see him but I run for a while, coz even half dead, I reckon I can outrun the Ape. I fall down in the grass and just stay there until the yelling stops. I wait for the whirring sound of grass heads on the car, but it never comes. Of course, the Ape's not coming for me. Ma left me. I cry, coz I figure out I'm still waiting, deep in my heart, for her to come looking for me, but I'm

176

too tired and too dry for tears. I get up and keep walking, hoping I'm not walking in circles, hoping the wide yellow sea hasn't tricked me again.

The next fence, I just kind of fall over it. I'm in an orchard all overgrown with grass and trees dry and shaggy with dead leaves. I think something has happened to my farm while I been gone. That it's this now. All dried up and all the people moved on. I run on staggering, wobbling legs, and soon I'm in an open yellow field again.

Then a new kind of roar. The roar of a tractor, just like Foreman rides. I lift my hand against the sun and try to see, but my knees give out and I flop sideways onto the ground. I sit and look into the sun and Applejoy yells, "P! Peony!" and then Foreman is there, scooping me up, making AJ pour water into my mouth. Then I'm on the tractor safe in Foreman's lap with AJ pouring water on my face as we bounce across the paddocks.

"How did you find me?" I ask and my voice croaks out like an old goat.

AJ laughs. "The truck drivers saw you," he says. "They said a girl with fluffy dark hair was walking the fields for days. I been searching and watching from the hill. I saw you coming. You's only on the next farm over!"

I try to smile but my lips crack.

Foreman delivers me down into Gramps's arms. I press my face into his smoky shirt chest, and he whispers, "Peony, my sweet honey girl." And I know I am home.

AIN'T ENOUGH
TO GO ROUND

It takes me a few days to get better. Foreman drops in some cans of fish, and some bandages to cover my grazed feet from the flies, and Gramps makes me drink lots and eat lots, and washes my feet every day. He says the Ape was no man at all to steal a small girl, and he worries for Rosie. I tell him Rosie is mean for hurting Mags and taking me away, and he shouldn't worry about her. But he says he will always worry about his little girls.

"Rosie's a grown-up and she shouldn't be so greedy for stuff she can't have all the time," I say. "And she gave up on us. She pretends like we're not her family anymore."

Gramps rubs his fingers through my hair, and kisses

179

my forehead and says, "Rosie always thought her life would be different. She has dreams and she can't shake them, never mind that the world's changed and we all have simpler dreams now."

I shrug. "This is our home. This shed is nice."

Gramps hugs me close. "Hear that?" he asks.

His heart thuds strong and slow through his smoky shirt. I nod, my ear scraping up and down against his shirt.

"That's where your home is," he says. "In my heart, and you'll always be there. You and Mags and Rosie."

Autumn sets in hard and sudden, with cold, cold nights, and Foreman finds a couple more old potbelly stoves for the families that moved in over packing time and want to stay on. We help them collect materials from around the packing shed and nail it up to make proper sheds like the rest of us.

Pomegranate is leaning on the shed opposite, standing on one foot with the other tap-tap-tapping to some tune in her head. When I put a bit of wood up against one of the new sheds, I turn and give her a scowl for not helping.

"My sister's gonna get me a job in the city," she says, like maybe that makes her super-cherries.

"Cha! Stupid," I say.

She drops her foot and stands up off the shed. "Why?"

"Those Urbs bossing you about, making you do stupid jobs they could just do themselves," I say.

Pomz frowns like she don't believe me.

"Why you wanna go and give up your bee vest for that?" I ask. "You wanted to bee for such a long time."

"Yeah, but I did that, now I wanna get some money like my sister. She can buy stuff. Nice shoes and lip gloss and chocolate and stuff."

"Cha!" I say and shake my head, and turn away to adjust the wood against the new shed.

"What?" Pomz says.

"You wanna give up your bee vest for rubbish," I say.

"It's not rubbish," she says and she takes a deep breath. "What's it like in the city, P?"

I turn back and put my hands on my hips. "Don't go," I say.

"Go stomp yourself, pest," Pomz says.

"Alright, go to the city, stupid bee," I say back. "I'll take your bee vest if you don't want it."

Pomz who's taller than me by a squeak fronts up to me like she might wanna hit me.

"Only reason you'd be in my sister's face is if you

181

want me to break all your fingers for you," Mags says as she's dragging a bit of wood past.

Pomz stomps off.

I grin coz it's good to be back in a family. I run and help Mags with her bit of wood which is real heavy.

AJ's been keen to hear the stories about the Pasquales and all their rich-people things, but Mags has been just getting up and leaving, acting all busy, like she don't want to hear about where Ma was working. And after how Ma was last time she saw Mags, I understand why.

"You know Ma was wrong to treat you so bad," I say. Now I got Mags stuck on the other end of a huge lump of wood, she has to hear me out.

"It wasn't about you. Ma dumped me too," I say. "Before I left the city. She dumped me cold for that Ape."

Mags and me drop the wood out the front of the new shed and Mags sighs and looks out down the row of sheds.

"Ma's like one of those big yellow lemons," she says. "You think it's gotta be good coz it's so big and has perfect skin but when you cut it in half you find out its skin is so thick there's just a tiny bit of pulp inside and that it just ain't got enough juice to go around."

I nod, coz I been caught out choosing the biggest

lemon when Foreman's tree has too many and he hands them round. It makes you feel real stupid to be tricked by a lemon.

Mags hugs me and then shoves me away, so I almost fall down as she takes off running and laughing back up to the packing shed junk pile.

Winter sets in even harder. Boxes of second-hand clothes get delivered from the city and we look through them all to find warm jackets and long pants. Mags scores a pair of boots with soft fur lining and she dances around like she's all super-cherries. And when she dances in those boots she don't even limp. She spins and leaps, head back laughing.

"You's so beautiful, Mags!" I yell and I think that Ma was so stupid to call Mags a gimp. Mags is stronger than all of us.

Pomz's sister comes home from the city for a visit and she just moans about the cold all the time. When she leaves, she takes Pomz back with her. Pomz walks past my shed beside her sister with her bag in her hand. She looks at me as she passes and I shake my head. She pokes her tongue out.

"She told me she's just gonna to try it for a month,"

Mags whispers after she goes past. "She'll be back before spring, I bet."

I shrug. "I'll look good in bee stripes," I say.

Mags pokes me in the side. "This spring for sure."

THE LONG BLACK CAR

Spring is a lifetime away. A long slow cold winter away.
Some nights so cold, Mags comes crawling into my bed
bringing her blanket so we can double our blankets and
double our body heat.

Some days the sun sits so high and clear, it beats
back the winter just a little bit.

And on one of those days a long black car pulls up
the drive and Jonagold gets out and walks around and
opens the door and Esmeralda points her toe and steps
from the car, gliding with her head perched way up high
on her neck, and that's how I know she's still a bit scared
about being outside.

"Ez!" I yell and leave my sitting log beside the fire and run over to the car.

She grins. Mrs. Pasquale steps from the car behind her.

"Hello, Peony," she says. "I'm glad to see you made it home, safely."

"Yes, Ma'am," I say.

"Your mother came back for a little while but she wasn't well and she took her things and left with that man of hers," Mrs. Pasquale says and puts her lips together hard like she don't approve.

"Yeah," I agree and put my lips together hard too, coz I'm not approving even more.

"I didn't give her your pay. I have it here, and I wanted to make sure you got it because you were a real blessing to our family. Esmeralda is so much happier, and she is back at dance classes, and even going on school excursions, and now look at us! So far from home on our own excursion!" she says, waves her hand at the trees, then she holds out an envelope.

I smile at Ez. "You can give the money to my gramps," I say to Mrs. Pasquale. "I don't need it." I point down to the fire pit where Gramps is boiling up a pot of tea.

"Oh," Mrs. Pasquale says and takes careful, trit-trotting steps on her tottery heels towards the fire. Then she stops and looks back at me. "Peony, I've put a little extra in here, for helping Esmeralda. And even though you don't need it now, please spend it on something you do need, one day." She wobbles on her heels scratching at the gravel the rest of the way down to the fire pit, past Mags and AJ who have stopped to stare.

"Well," I say to Esmeralda, "do you want to try being a bee for real?"

"Yes!" Esmeralda says.

I grab her hand and tow her down to AJ. "AJ's our finest bee!" I tell her.

AJ's cheeks turn red and he kicks at the dirt with the toe of his second-hand sneaker.

"Aaj," I say. "Can we borrow your vest and a bee wand?"

AJ scoots off to his shed. He's back in a flash with his vest and an old bee wand that has lost its end.

I fit the vest over Esmeralda's shoulders. "You look just like a bee!" I say and grab her hand and tow her down to the orchard.

We pass Gramps who has Mrs. Pasquale perched on my log with a cup of tea in her hands. Her back is straight as a bee pole and she wears a stiff smile. Gramps is waving at Jonagold to come down for a cup of tea too.

We run, laughing, through the clear bright cold down to the apple trees with their thick old branches and weathered wood and not a leaf in sight. AJ runs after us and Mags follows along. Without the leaves to slow the sound, our noise carries like it can travel around the whole world.

I help Esmeralda up the tree, and she stands on the branch, clinging to the trunk like a possum.

"Hey, Esmeralda Pasquale! Stand tall, you's the last honey bee!" I yell.

Esmeralda, lifts her chin and stretches her neck, she levers her shoes off and lets them fall to the ground, then she points her toe in her fluffy socks and tiptoes across the branch with her arms out for balance.

Mags claps her hands and I do too. AJ joins in. Esmeralda bobs to each of us. Then sits on the branch and slides off to the ground. She pulls her shoes back on.

"You forgot to try the wand," I say.

"No way," she says. "Being a bee is really hard. I can't balance and wave a pole." She pulls the vest off, folds it carefully, like she understands how special it is, and gives it back to AJ.

"Thank you," she says.

AJ blushes again.

Esmeralda turns back to me. "Ivy made us sandwiches. She said you like lots of butter."

I laugh.

Mrs. Pasquale has to take phone calls so she sits in the car while Esmeralda opens the biggest container of sandwiches I've ever seen. She hands them all out to everyone around the fire and when AJ runs off to give his sandwich to his mum, she makes sure he has another one. He finally finds his voice then and squeaks out, "Thanks!"

The sandwiches are amazing. The bread is so soft and the fillings are all different, some creamy, some spicy. Mags and I keep comparing ours to try to guess what's in them. Esmeralda laughs at us and says things like, "It's ham, avo and mayo." Which makes Mags and me look at each other and laugh too coz "ham, avo and mayo" makes her voice sound silly and we have no idea what it is. Still it's fun to sit in the sun beside the fire and try lots of unusual tastes, and I'm happy Esmeralda has come to make a break from the long slow winter.

Esmeralda likes it when Mangojoy wakes up from his nap, and she gives him a sandwich too. First he hides his face in AJ's neck but then he takes the sandwich and cuddles it to his chest and licks the centre of it when he

189

thinks Esmeralda isn't looking, but she is and laughs at him and calls him a little mouse.

Then Mrs.Pasquale calls Esmeralda, "Come on, we've got a long trip home, and Jonagold will be tired."

Esmeralda stands and does one of her grandmother's twirls and bows low, with her hands gliding out like swallows taking off. Her hair swirls and slides over her shoulders.

Everyone claps coz she looks amazing and they don't know that she dances like her grandmother to feel brave.

I walk with her back to the car. "I'm happy you came to visit, Ez," I say.

Ez hugs me quickly. "I'll come see you again," she says. "You've got a nice farm."

"Yeah," I say like I'm already the foreman here.

Jonagold comes and holds the car door for her and she jumps into the car.

Mrs. Pasquale stops talking on her phone a moment to wave. "Thank you, Peony!"

Jonagold shuts the door, turns to me and winks. "Bye, Miss Peony Bee," he says.

AJ stands beside me as I watch the car crunch over the gravel and go back down the driveway.

"She was like some kind of princess," he whispers.

"Nah," I say. "She's just a funny, scared girl."

SUN-BLEACHED BONES

The winter drags its cold feet over our land, too lazy to move on. AJ's mum gets too sick to look after Mangojoy so Gramps brings him to live with us for a while. Every night, he rocks little MJ to sleep and says, "Hush, little man, you're all safe." Then he slides MJ into bed with me and I wrap him in my blanket and listen to his little fast breaths as he sleeps.

AJ's mum, Lily, gets sicker. No matter that Foreman gets the doctor out, and Gramps takes the cash money he has hid in our floor and gives it to the doctor for medicine. No matter that Foreman drops off lots of cans of fish, and Mags gives Lily all our eggs, and AJ keeps the

191

potbelly stove stoked hot day and night. We go to sleep each night listening to her coughing and rasping in the shed next door.

Then one quiet night I wake with Mangojoy tight up against me breathing his little sleeping breaths and Gramps rocking in his chair still saying, "Hush, little man, you're all safe." He says it over and over, and in the moonlight I see it's AJ curled up there on my gramps's lap. AJ who's become small and curled up like a baby.

In the morning when Mangojoy stirs, I get up and take him from the shed so the others can sleep. The fire that burned day and night at AJ's is just a trickle of smoke in the chimney and when I pull open the packing-crate door, Lily lies in the bunk with the blanket up over her face and her feet sticking out the bottom whiter than sun-bleached bones.

PAPER FLOWERS

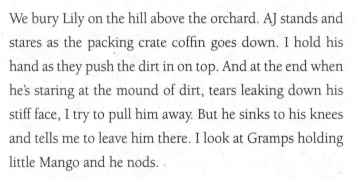

We bury Lily on the hill above the orchard. AJ stands and stares as the packing crate coffin goes down. I hold his hand as they push the dirt in on top. And at the end when he's staring at the mound of dirt, tears leaking down his stiff face, I try to pull him away. But he sinks to his knees and tells me to leave him there. I look at Gramps holding little Mango and he nods.

We walk down the hill and leave AJ sitting beside the dirt mound. I stand watching him, and I guess he's talking to her or something. Then he throws himself onto the mound and digs like a dog tunnelling into it.

"Gramps!" I yell and point. Gramps puts little MJ

down, pushes his tiny hand into mine and climbs the hill again and fetches AJ back. He carries him to our shed and rocks him in the chair till he's asleep. AJ sleeps in my bunk for two full days without moving.

Gramps lays little Mangojoy in there with him each night, and I sleep above with Mags. Then AJ is up and ready to work again. He pulls on his bee vest even though there are no blossoms and goes out with me and Mags to weed around the trees and look for pests. He makes sure all the possum sleeves are fitting the trees properly, and in the afternoon, he holds MJ's hand and walks him up and down the paths so the little boy is happy and tired out by the end of the day.

Foreman sees him working real hard and tells him he's a good kid.

Applejoy smiles, and then I know he's going to be alright. So I relax, and start talking to him properly like he's my friend again and not a broken person. And even though he doesn't answer me right away, like the old Aaj used to, day after day he finds his way back to himself.

I make flowers from packing paper left on the packing shed floor and I tie them up with wire. I give them to AJ and he smiles like maybe they're real. He takes the flowers and little MJ on his hip and walks all the way up the hill to Lily's grave for the first time since they buried her there. I stay at the bottom and watch him in case he does that thing where he digs like a crazy dog again, but he sits there for a long time and he talks to Mangojoy and points to the grave. When he comes back down he seems calmer.

"Thanks for the flowers, P," he says. "Ma loved them."

"I'll make some more next week," I promise.

BIG AS A QUEEN

Winter is all about managing grass and pruning the trees and keeping warm. There's not so much work for us to do. AJ, Mags and I run screaming through the cold morning air to the bathrooms at the bottom of the hill every morning, play silly games in the hut with old Urb toys that usually have bits missing so we have to be smart to work out new ways to use them, or carve our own bits from wood. We play with little Mango and keep him from burning himself on the stove. Every afternoon we go out to collect the prunings from under the fruit trees and stack them up for firewood. When the weather's dry, we pull the grass from around the tree trunks. If it's wet we don't. The cold bites wet fingers real bad. On wet days, we sit in our shed and beg Gramps for stories about the old times before the famine and what kinds of food he remembers and the real house he lived in when he was a boy. His bathroom was in the house and he had electricity for lights and taps and sinks inside. Mags and AJ think that's super-cherries. I think they'd both scream if they saw Esmeralda's house.

Applejoy and I sneak over to Foreman's house and peek in the windows, coz AJ's never been in an actual real house that he remembers. I kneel in the garden and let AJ stand on my back to look in the window. When it's my turn, all I see standing on AJ's back, is a room with an enormous bed in it and the flash of Foreman's wife's hips as she dashes across the window in front of me. She runs out yelling and screaming for us to get out of her yard. We run, heads down so she can't tell Foreman what we look like, and we hoot and laugh when we are safely back in the orchard.

"Boz's bed is as big as our whole shed!" I tell AJ.

"That's coz his wife is as big as a queen," AJ says and nods like he thinks Foreman got the bed made specially to fit the hips of his wife.

"Cha!" I say and push him over in the wet grass and run down the hill.

Foreman is away from the farm a lot over winter and when I ask him where he goes he says, "I'm learning about bees."

I laugh and say, "You already know all the bees."

He taps the side of his nose and winks.

Foreman is good with people. He's gruff as a wild billy goat, and sweet as a cherry blossom, and he takes care of his people real good. I'm gonna be just like him.

THE BEST SURPRISE

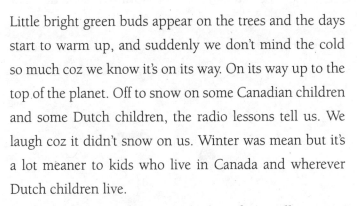

Little bright green buds appear on the trees and the days start to warm up, and suddenly we don't mind the cold so much coz we know it's on its way. On its way up to the top of the planet. Off to snow on some Canadian children and some Dutch children, the radio lessons tell us. We laugh coz it didn't snow on us. Winter was mean but it's a lot meaner to kids who live in Canada and wherever Dutch children live.

AJ and me are first with the bare feet, walking over the cold hard mud, not wincing one bit and telling each other it don't hurt at all. Why's cold feet feel every little bump on the ground so much? The other farm kids watch us but keep their shoes on a while longer.

Foreman comes and talks to Gramps. They sit on packing crates next to an open fire outside and they're deep in conversation. Gramps nods and smiles and stands up and shakes Foreman's hand.

"What's that about?" I ask when Gramps comes back grinning from ear to ear.

"That's a surprise, sweet honey. That's the best surprise for you," and I know that Foreman is going to make me a bee straight out this spring. Maybe he's had news that Pomz ain't coming back. That'd be cherries. I'm ten and Applejoy is almost eleven so with two bees in the family we're going to be earning loads of food to keep everyone fed.

LAVENDER

I'm out checking pears, sitting in a tree, hunting for bud-eating bugs, when the bus stops way down on the road. I watch, hoping that Pomegranate won't step out and ruin my plans for bee. Only one person gets off. A woman. She stands in a way I know, shoulders rolled forwards. She's dragging a big case on wheels and she looks around when the bus leaves, like she ain't never been here before. As she sets off at a slow pace up our road, I jump from the tree and run down the hill towards her. I give her the names of all the women I know, and none stick. Part of me wishes it was Ma, finally come to her senses, but that will never happen.

I'm real close, close enough even to hear her puffing, when she lifts her head and looks at me and stops me dead. I pull out my bug spike and hold it out in front of me.

"Well!" she says. And she looks like Lily. Lily, AJ's mum, dead and buried on the hill.

"You come back from the dead to take your children away with you?" I ask.

The woman drops her case and grabs her knees and laughs, and laughs. "Oh," she says and grabs a breath. "'Splains why you look like you've seen a ghost!"

Now I look at her, her face is fatter than Lily's and she's larger all over and she has bits of grey hair over her ears. She slaps the tears from her cheeks.

"At least I know I'm at the right place," she says. "I'm Lavender. I'm Lily's older sister."

I tilt my head and study her. "You come to visit AJ and Mangojoy?" I ask, coz if she's come to take them away I might go ahead and poke her with this pest spike anyway.

"Well," she says, and slaps her thigh. "I have to tell you a story. My own boy is grown and working for himself now and I thought, 'I wonder how my little sister is doing with her boy? I got some money I could send her.' So I make some calls and wind up talking to the Foreman of this orchard. He tells me poor Lily is no more, and there's not one boy, there's two! He also tells me Applejoy is a fine young man who's already a bee and has a nice shed, and he wouldn't want to see him go, but that an old man was taking care of Applejoy and Mangojoy and they were in need of some help. So Foreman tells me if I can survive on what I got put away, and some picking and packing money then why don't I get out of the city? And I thought, why don't I? So here I am. Ready to move in and hoping like mad AJ thinks that's a good idea."

I smile and nod. Lavender's real cherries. It's not often an adult will stop to tell a kid a whole story like that, and she's a real good sister to Lily. This is the kind of thing me and Mags will do for each other one day if we have to.

"AJ will love it," I tell her. "Coz that's what you do for family."

"I reckon," Lavender says.

I take the handle of her bag and help her drag it on its slip-sliding little plastic wheels all the way up to the farm, and down past our place to AJ's shed.

Gramps comes out holding Mangojoy and we tell him the story.

Everyone's happy and grinning and Aunty Lav is

bouncing a happy MJ on her hip when AJ arrives home from working with the bees. He stands and stares and his eyes fill with water that leaks out the sides. His chin sets to wobbling and puckers up real bad with little white dimples in the middle like the muscles there are out of control.

I run over to him, in case he thinks it's a fat ghost of Lily too.

"It's your aunt Lavender," I say quickly. "She's come to live. She's come to help."

AJ hitches in a couple of breaths and runs stumbling to her, he wraps his arms tight around her middle like he's never gonna let go.

"Hey, now, my boy," she says softly and wraps an arm around him and rocks him from side to side.

Gramps pats his hair. "You're all safe, little man," he says.

"You're looking real smart and grown-up in your bee vest," Lav says. She passes MJ back to Gramps and gets down on her knees and holds AJ up and looks hard in each of his eyes. "I want to move into your shed and take care of you and Mangojoy. Is that something you want too?"

AJ nods and sniffs and keeps nodding so hard, we all laugh.

We spend the rest of the day tidying up AJ's shed and

getting the fire roaring to dry it out properly so Lavender can move in.

Gramps still rocks Mangojoy to sleep that night but then he delivers him next door to Lavender. I miss his little fast breaths in the night, even though he has been sleeping with AJ on the bottom bunk since Lily died, and I've been sleeping on top with Mags.

HONEY BABY

Foreman's there the next morning waiting for me and AJ to come out of our sheds. He's holding a bundle of white though, not a nice striped bee vest for me.

"Peony and Applejoy," he says all formal. AJ and I look at each other real quick to see if we know what's goin' on. "Give me your vests."

I peel out of my green pest vest right away and hand it over, but AJ's standing there and looking down at his hard-earned stripes, not wanting to give them up, and I don't know why he should. I wouldn't give up my stripes if I had them. Specially if I'd never done anything wrong.

"Trust me, son," Foreman says and holds out his hand. AJ peels off his vest and folds it carefully and lays it on Foreman's hand.

"You two are the toughest, most dedicated farm kids I have," he says.

Mags sticks her head out to see what's happening. Foreman sees her and smiles. "Apart from Magnolia, but I need her to train up my pests." He looks back at me and AJ. "I have a special job for you two. I want you to be bee-keepers."

"To train the bees and tell them what to do?" I ask.

Foreman laughs. "No," he says. "Bee-keeping is an ancient profession, which you'll be able to use anywhere once you're trained. We're bringing real bees back to the orchard."

I lift my eyebrows at him. I'm trying to get my head to stop screaming at me that I'll never bee. I was so close!

"Cha!" I grumble and Foreman throws up a hand in my face.

"Don't you give me that look, Peony. This is better. Way better than being a bee." He tilts his head towards me like he's giving me time to calm down or he might yell at me. "This is the future."

He holds out the white bundles. One for me and one

for AJ. I unfold mine. A white vest, and a white hat with netting on the brim. Long white gloves fall to the dirt and I snatch them up and wipe them on my trousers.

"The first hive arrives today and another next week. I'm going to train you in how to care for them, and how to collect honey—"

"Honey?" I ask and wonder how someone like me gets to be the one to touch something so precious.

Foreman laughs and nods. "Honey. Real honey. And if you do a good job and the bees flourish, we can set up other hives ourselves and eventually have lots of them all over the orchard."

Applejoy pulls on his white vest and hat and he remembers his manners and holds out his hand.

"Thank you, sir!" he says and Foreman shakes his hand then offers his hand to me.

"Yes, Boz!" I say. "Thank you." I grip his hand real firm and shake it.

Foreman looks serious at both of us. "I trust you two. I trust you to learn quickly and work hard and to work for me long enough to repay the training. Your family is well-settled here." Foreman points at Gramps who is standing behind us, and Lavender who is leaning in the doorway of AJ's shed holding Mangojoy and smiling. "And you are young so you won't run off and marry anyone in a nearby orchard anytime soon."

AJ and I look at each other and laugh at that stupid idea.

"After two years I should be able to start paying you a wage in cash. Come up to the driveway when you hear the truck," Foreman says and strides away. "You start work today!"

AJ and I pull on all the gear and slap each other with the white gloves, giggling like mad.

Soon enough, there's the roar of a motor and crunching gravel in the driveway, so we run flat out. But it's only a dented-up old car.

It stops and the Ape gets out. He sees me and tries to look under my new white hat. "Peony, is that you?" he asks.

I back up into AJ. "Who's that?" AJ asks.

"The Ape man!" I whisper. AJ grabs my hand like there's no way he's going to let go.

I'm brave with AJ beside me, so I yell, "Where's my ma?"

The Ape man lifts his hands to the air, shakes his head like he's got some story. But before he can get to it, Foreman arrives in his white hat and gloves and strides right at the Ape man, picks him up and throws him back against the car. He punches him so hard in the mouth, a dirty red smear is left on Foreman's new white glove.

"Don't you come on my farm ever!" Foreman yells. "Don't you touch my farm kids!"

The Ape straightens up holding his jaw in one hand. He holds the other hand out to stop Foreman from hitting him again. "I won't!" he says and he jerks his thumb in the back window of his car.

Foreman looks there and steps back.

"Ma!" I yell, coz I'm scared that the Ape has beat up Ma and left her in the back of the car. I start forwards with AJ still hanging on to my hand, to find Ma, to beat up the Ape right back if I have to.

"I can't take it," the Ape says. "I came to drop it off with its grandad, that's all."

"Where's her mother?" Foreman says like he's ready to hit Ape again.

"Dead. Dead and buried," Ape says. "Last thing she said was, bring her here. Said the baby needed a real family." He slides past Foreman and pulls open the back door, reaches in and pulls out a baby wrapped in a pink blanket. He presses the baby into Foreman's arms, runs and jumps in the driver's side and backs quickly down the drive, turns the car around and takes off, showering us with stones and dust.

Foreman unfolds from shielding the baby and turns to look at me.

AJ still has my gloved hand in his and he squeezes it. Now we both lost mothers, but I got used to the idea mine wasn't ever coming back a whole season ago, so my heart's not breaking the way Applejoy's did. I just got to get used to the idea that she's really gone for good. That's not breaking my heart, that's just putting a cold empty hole in it. A Ma-shaped hole that was already there, but now will never close over. I blink the tears from my eyes.

Foreman steps over and holds the baby out to me. "Cha!" he says and shakes his head.

I take off my gloves and tuck them into my waistband.

"Peony," Foreman says. "I think this is your little sister and maybe your ma is dead."

"Yes, Boz," I say, and take the baby and cuddle her and stroke her cheek. So soft, so small and beautiful with her little dark lashes, and little apple-blossom bud mouth. I smile coz I'm pleased that Ma knew to send her to us. She finally knew that the best place was here.

"I'll come down and explain it to your gramps," Foreman says. Then he sighs and says, "Your poor ma."

211

"I tried real hard to bring her home," I say, and Foreman looks at me and pats me on top of my bee-keeping hat.

"Good bee-keeper," he says.

Foreman reaches our shed first, and Gramps comes out holding little Mangojoy, who squirms to get down on the too-cold ground with his bare feet. Foreman grips Gramps's shoulder and delivers the news about Ma, which sends Gramps's knees weak. Foreman grabs him as Mangojoy slides to the ground, and the little boy runs towards AJ who scoops him up and shows him the baby.

Mags comes out and props up the other side of Gramps.

Then Foreman points to where I stand waiting, with the tiny baby in my arms. He whispers something softly. Gramps looks at Foreman like he can't believe it. He pulls himself up and hurries over with Mags and looks at the little baby.

"So much like Rosie," he says, his red-rimmed eyes blinking through tears. His rough, wrinkled finger reaches out as if he wants to touch the baby but he's afraid she's not real.

"Ma knew," I tell him. "Ma knew to send her to us, to her family. She finally knew."

Gramps nods. He gets it.

"Let's call her Honey," I say.

"Sweet and precious like honey," Gramps whispers.

"Sweet and precious like family," I whisper back.

Then a truck roars and crunches into the driveway with a box wrapped in see-through plastic on the back. The box sits there, white and blue and yellow, bright and real and waiting.

"Bee-keepers, we have work to do!" Foreman says in his normal bossy voice, dragging us back to what needs doing.

"Yes, Boz!" AJ and I say together. I hand over baby Honey to Gramps, and AJ takes little Mango to Lavender who's standing in her doorway, and we run laughing and tingling, my gloves flapping at my waist, up to the truck.

ACKNOWLEDGMENTS

In a crazy, crazy year, I thank my family, friends, writing buddies and work colleagues for their patient, unwavering support. Thanks to Susannah and the team at Allen & Unwin for loving Peony and bringing her story alive. And to all the foremen on all the farms, why weren't you ever as nice as Boz?

ABOUT THE AUTHOR

Bren MacDibble was raised on farms all over New Zealand, so is an expert about being a kid on the land. After twenty years in Melbourne, Bren recently sold everything, and now lives and works on a bus traveling around Australia. *How to Bee*, her first children's novel, won the Children's Book Council Book of the Year Award for Younger Readers, the New South Wales Premier's Literary Award Patricia Wrightson Prize for Children's Literature and the New Zealand Book Awards Wright Family Foundation Esther Glen Award for Junior Fiction. She has also written the middle-grade novel *The Dog Runner*.

www.macdibble.com